STORMY RANGE

Mean Meaker and his mob were on the loose, all for gunning down the marshal and getting their hands on the Hardin brothers' killer. The youngest Hardin, however, had escaped death. Clem was the runt of the litter, the kid who didn't want trouble and who was trying to make the Ladder Ranch stand for decency in Kettle Creek. But he didn't stand a chance. He was a Hardin and the men of Kettle had long memories. They had taken a lot from the Hardins, too much to forget. So the word went out: get Clem Hardin. Cut him down from behind if need be—just get him!

STORMY RANGE

Dwight Bennett Newton

WESTERNS

First published 1951
by
Doubleday & Company, Inc.

This hardback edition 1995
by Chivers Press
by arrangement with the author.
Reprinted by arrangement with
Golden West Literary Agency

ISBN 0 7451 4638 4

British Library Cataloguing in Publication Data available

Printed and bound in Great Britain by
Redwood Books, Trowbridge, Wiltshire

STORMY RANGE

THERE WAS nothing that day to indicate a storm was about to break over the Kettle Creek country. It was a mellow summer's afternoon, such as often hangs on after fall has started. The sun had considerable warmth, and it was brassy against a high haze that was smoke from a forest fire far back in the timbered hills. The smell of the fire was in the air too—a faint irritant to sting a man's nostrils and start him grumbling. Perhaps that smoke, rubbing against tempers already raw, would have its own tiny part in the events that were to shape and break open the still quiet.

Along toward three, the Hardin brothers came jingling into Tilden town from their Ladder ranch, on some errand or other that was never to be completed. Big Noah, the oldest, with heavy shoulders and wings of gray in the thick black hair that curled at his temples; Japheth, a smaller edition of his brother, with the same dark beard and the same harsh, perpetual scowl. And Clement Hardin, who did not much resemble the other two because he took his features from his mother, dead Sam Hardin's second wife.

Noah and Japheth could remember their stepmother, even now, as small and fair and sweet, and always a little frightened of her great bearlike husband and his two surly sons. But Clem Hardin could not remember her at all, because Sarah Hardin had died in bearing him.

They came off the hills and into the dusty crisscross of Tilden's streets, and the town was silent around them.

Noah scowled at the sun-scoured lifts of false-fronted buildings. He said: "I'm headin' for Cal's first and wash this damn smoke out of my throat. Stuff stings to beat hell."

"Especially," said Japheth, "since a man ain't hardly allowed even to get him a drink out of old Kettle Creek no more."

"*That* state of things may change mighty blamed quick," Noah muttered cryptically. He added, "You coming with us, kid?"

"I don't reckon," said Clement Hardin.

He knew they didn't want him. His half brothers never did. They felt they had their reasons for hating him, and Clem had grown to accept this almost without resentment. He said now, by way of excuse, "My horse rides like he had a loose shoe. I'd better run him around to the stable and let Limp have a glance at it."

"All right."

The other pair rode on to Cal's, and Clem Hardin watched them dismount there, throw reins loosely across the tie rail, and step down to their ankles in white powdery dust. Heavy cowhides thumped against warped plankings as they crossed the boardwalk and went up the three broad steps to the saloon's porch. The doors stood open. Japheth halted to let his elder brother enter first.

Once, when big Sam was alive, both boys had stood aside for the father they resembled so strongly. Three heavy, black-bearded figures they had been, with shoulders that rolled forward of their own weight, and a capacity for Cal's poison booze that astonished other men when the trio larruped into town for a Saturday night's celebration. In those days old Sam had ruled his sons with a hand of iron that never let an inch of slack into the reins. Maybe that explained what had happened since the time, two years ago, when Sam topped his last wild one in the Ladder corral and got himself stomped to death. Maybe a little more tact in his handling of Noah and Japheth, and the respect that had belonged to Ladder iron in Sam's day wouldn't have turned to hatred and suspicion now.

Clem had this thought, a little vaguely, watching his half brothers tramp inside the saloon. He was frowning over it as he rode on along the street, heading for the livery.

The faded sign above the tobacco shop reminded him he was out of Bull Durham and he reined in there. And coming out a moment later, stuffing the sack of makin's into his shirt pocket, he encountered Bob Fox on the sidewalk and the two exchanged a solemn greeting. A tall man, Fox—six foot five, with no meat at all to pad his stringy frame. The town marshal's badge hung like a weight, pinned to his shirt front, but the burden that sagged his shoulders and put a faintly beaten look on the old man's face was that of the years, and of the large family he had managed somehow to bring up on the meager salary the city council begrudged him.

"Howdy, Clement," he said, smiling tiredly. "Sally know you're in town?"

"Just rode in, Bob. I was fixing to come by a little later."

"Better do that."

The marshal's mild eyes smiled at him, innocently calculating; a poor man with four daughters could hardly have completely candid relations with the young men he met from day to day. And Bob Fox liked Clem, both as an individual and as a prospective son-in-law; liked the cut of him, the honest, direct look of his blue eyes.

Of course Clem Hardin was only a youngster—just turned twenty. His frame wasn't completely filled out, and his hands tended to reddish, bony knuckles, and he likely wasn't shaving regular yet. But Bob Fox had his knowledge of men, and he thought Clem would do.

Moreover, Sally liked him. Sally had known him all her life, and grown up with him. And her approval was enough for Bob.

They spent a few minutes in range talk, idly discussing Ladder affairs, the late summer drought, the stinging haze of foothill smoke. Then Clem got his horse and rode on around to the livery barn, to have that loose shoe tended to; this was at three-twenty. It was a quarter hour later, perhaps, that the two gunshots slapped out within the boxlike interior of Cal's saloon.

Any disturbance at all was such a rare occasion in the somnolent peace of this town that it was doubly startling to hear the quick, violent ripping of the explosions. Marshal Fox, playing checkers now with the proprietor of the tobacco shop, gave a start and his mild eyes widened, locked with those of the tobacconist for a frozen second of alarm.

"Good God almighty!" breathed the old proprietor.

"Sounded like they both come from one gun, didn't it?" The marshal's voice was hushed, as though awed by the dying echoes. But then he straightened his long, skinny frame and, turning from the counter, strode hurriedly across the dark storeroom. One bony hand checked the low-riding gun and holster as he went; that hand held a small trembling.

Bob Fox was as brave as any ordinary officeholder. But it had been so very long since this job of his had involved any possibility of danger that for an instant he seemed able to think of nothing but his wife, and his brood of four girls.

A moment later he was in the empty street, staring across the dust toward Cal's saloon. No movement showed at first. Then, stumbling like one drunk or dazed, a man came through the wide, propped-open door of Cal's.

He was Nat Brophy, and he owned one of the little nester places neighboring the Hardin brothers' ranch along Kettle Creek. He reeled to the edge of the porch, halted there, and set one hand against a wooden roof support and leaned on it. In that hand was a six-shooter. Its muzzle still leaked a dribble of smoke.

The town marshal started across the street at a run; he had a queer gait that lifted his long legs high with every stride. He saw other people beginning to move into sight now, at doors and windows. When he halted at the foot of the porch steps he was so gauntly tall he hardly needed to lift his head to meet the level of Brophy's dull, staring eyes on the stoop above him.

"My God, Nat," he demanded harshly, "what happened?"

There was no answer. Brophy stood as he was, slack-jawed, eyes seemingly out of focus. Impatiently Bob Fox went up the steps, shoved past him, and crossed the porch with a single stride. But in the doorway he hauled up, horror tightening like a hand upon him.

Stench of powder smoke hung foul in the breathless air. And crumpled on the splintered boards lay all that was mortal of Japheth and Noah Hardin.

Noah was on his back, one thick boot across the brass railing, sightless eyes turned up in what looked like a stare of surprise. His brother was crumpled half across his body; Bob Fox could see the smear of blood between his shoulders, and the ugly thought registered: *Shot in the back!*

Except for the dead, the room's only occupant was Cal Wormer himself, behind the bar. The bald-headed man was gripping the edge of the mahogany with stubby fingers, and his horrified stare met Bob Fox's above the carnage on the floor.

"I couldn't stop it!" he gasped, his head shaking spasmodically. "I couldn't do nothing! Nat Brophy just stepped into the door with his gun out and began shooting, not even makin' a sound to warn 'em . . ." He added, "I ain't saying the Hardins didn't maybe have something like this comin' to 'em, but to get it that way——" He choked off, speech failing him.

Marshal Fox heeled around, went out again to where Brophy stood leaning against the wooden pillar as though in a kind of trance. It took a nudge at his elbow and his own name, spoken harshly, to bring him out of it. "Nat! I'm talkin' to you!"

Brophy turned then and, when he saw who it was, jerked away from the marshal and started to bring his gun level, bellowing wildly, "Keep clear of me! Keep clear away, you hear, or——"

A bony hand, clamping over his wrist, twisted and sent the gun clattering down the broad steps. "You fool!" cried the marshal. "You gone out of your head?"

"No!" Brophy shouted it on a rising note of frenzy. "I know what I'm doin'. I've saved this range from bein' plunged into bloody war."

"You've done murder, you mean!"

"It ain't murder to shoot down a mad dog that needs it. Them Hardins! We tried to get along with them! We all tried—all of us who was neighbors of that Ladder spread. We took more off them and their tough crew than it's right a white man should. I tell you——"

Bob Fox only shook his head. There was still a little of the sick horror in him which sight of the carnage inside the saloon had put there. "You don't have to tell me anything," he pointed out dryly. "You can keep all your talk for the jury, when you go up for trial at the county seat."

"Trial?" Nat Brophy repeated the word in a dazed voice, as though its meaning failed to register. The marshal's lean face hardened in a grimace.

"Certainly! Didn't it occur to you that you'd go to jail for this? I'm putting you under arrest for murder."

Someone said, "No, you ain't, Bob!"

The marshal's head lifted slowly, swiveled in a long, searching glance as he sought out the speaker. For the first time he became conscious of the crowd that had gathered. Cal stood silent in the door of his saloon, wide paunch all but filling it, his face still ashen gray and sweat-beaded. The saloon man was staring past Fox, and the latter turned, put his look upon the men grouped below him on the walk. He knew them all—nesters to a man, and neighbors of Nat Brophy's. He located their spokesman without difficulty.

"Watch yourself, Peterson," he warned curtly.

Blond Tom Peterson said, "This is our affair. Brophy struck for all of us that's been feeling the pressure from Ladder."

Fox's eyes narrowed. "Then you maybe knew that he was gonna do this? Maybe you even drew straws to see who got the job of gunning down the Hardins—in the back?"

"No!" the other replied emphatically, as a dangerous stiffening went through the men about him. "We knew nothin' about it—but it's done, and now we'll stand by Nat. It was either the Hardins or us, Bob. It was a storm that's been building ever since the day they signed Val Meeker and his tough crew, and brought them in here to shove us off of Kettle Creek." He added, "You heard what happened during the night, didn't you?"

The marshal frowned. "No."

"Our fences were cut and Ladder stock pushed through the gaps!" Peterson's voice lifted angrily. "Now maybe you see the pass things have come to. The lot of us met here in town today to try and form some common plan of action—and then Nat Brophy, with no more'n two bullets, solved our problem for us. You gonna go in the face of that? You gonna buck the will of men who've been your friends—or is the law putting its weight on the side of a range-hog outfit like the Ladder iron?"

There was no answer for a minute. Bob Fox looked over the faces of the men below him and sensed their common attitude. He even found a certain amount of danger in it. It was up to him to decide.

Nat Brophy seemed to think he knew what the marshal's decision would be. A little of his confidence came back and a hint of a smile touched his narrow features. "Bob ain't a fool. Get your broncs, boys. I'll be riding out with you in a few minutes."

The marshal's jaw hardened. What was happening to this town, anyway, and this range, that the processes of law should have come to stand for so little? Like any other man, he had watched the storm clouds gathering, knowing they would break and sweep this foothill country with their fury. But he hadn't known that it would come so soon—or that it would take this form.

He had foreseen that men would die, but somehow it had never occurred to him that the Hardins themselves —the boot-tough, heavy-handed brothers, with a bunkhouse full of hired guns to back them up—would be the first to fall. Or that men normally honest and law-abiding would now be defying him to arrest a murderer in the plain course of his duty.

Fox, of course, was no more than a town officer, without jurisdiction beyond the limits of Tilden's dusty streets. But it was ominous that he had heard no word, until this moment, of the doings on Kettle Creek range the night before. He remembered suddenly that he had talked to young Clement not an hour ago, without any mention of these things being made. Somehow he felt disappointment at that. But then, he thought, *Clem Hardin couldn't have known that Meeker was riding last night. He couldn't have been a party to such doings.*

Now he looked at these nesters, saw the false confidence beginning to build in them. He said slowly, "One thing I reckon you've forgotten."

"Yeah?"

"What do you think Val Meeker's gonna do when he learns about Jap and Noah?"

He saw that thought strike home. There was a silence before someone suggested, without conviction, "Aw, he and his bunch will pull out as soon as they know their jobs are gone——"

"Think so?" Bob Fox countered coldly. "You really figure men like that would tuck tail and run, without first tryin' to settle for the murder of the men who paid them gun wages?"

All at once fear had a hold of Nat Brophy. "I'll keep out of their way!" he promised, in a quick panic. "I'll hit for the hills! Take some food along, lie low for a few days——"

"And they'd look for you," the lawman pointed out in the same inexorable tone. "They'd hunt high and low. And naturally the first place they'd look would be your homestead. Your wife will be there—alone, Brophy. Had you forgot about that?"

Obviously he had. He hauled up as though struck across the face. "God!" he exclaimed hoarsely. "What—what am I gonna do?"

"I'll tell you," said the marshal. "You'll do just what I said in the first place. You're coming along with me—to jail!"

"*No!*"

"It's a nice tight little building," Fox pointed out patiently. "Ain't ever held much but a drunk or two in my time, but nobody's gonna break out of it—or into it, either. Not even those Ladder toughs."

Tom Peterson broke in before Brophy could answer. "Maybe he's right, Nat. They'll leave your wife alone if they know Kate isn't hiding you. And should they make a play to take you out of the jail, me and the rest of the boys will help the marshal stand them off. We promise we'll never let 'em get you!"

"But I—I——" Brophy looked about wildly, as though watching doors of escape closing on him. "I tell you I don't want to go to jail! I'd go mad. I thought you were my friends!"

"It's only temporary, and it's for your own damn good." Peterson was a man who could not be budged once his mind was fastened on a thing. He stooped, got Brophy's gun from under the edge of the sidewalk where it had skidded. "I'll take charge of this, Marshal."

"No! Wait! *Wait!*"

Babbling excited protests, Brophy tried to fight as they moved to head him for the tiny boxlike structure that was the jail. But Tom Peterson's hand was clamped onto one arm and the marshal's to the other. The crowd parted to let them through, and three other Kettle Creek men went with them, boots beating a ragged thunder from the warped sidewalk plankings. And all their faces were determined, and they quickly stopped bothering to argue with Brophy's pleadings.

Bob Fox used his key; they had to drag Brophy across the small front office, shove him into one of the two cell rooms. As the door clanged Brophy seized the bars and shook them wildly, hair streaming into his sweaty face. "Let me out of here!"

"For the love of God, shut up!" blond Peterson rapped

at him. "You got nothing to worry about, understand? We'll tell Kate what's happened, so she'll know. And you'll be out of here in no time—just as soon as we see what that hardcase Ladder crowd is going to do."

Turning the key in the lock, Bob Fox said nothing, but he had his reservations as to that. He hadn't figured on Brophy's own friends helping get the man behind bars, but this had taken him beautifully past a very tight corner, and now that the killer was where he belonged, Fox meant for him to stay there—to stand trial for murder. That was the law. Brophy might or might not be convicted; especially doubtful if the case went before a Kettle Creek jury. Maxwell, the county seat, would have to worry about that. As town marshal, Fox had no further duty than to hold Brophy in his jail until he could get word for a deputy sheriff to come and pick him up.

Stepping out into the hazy stillness, Fox stretched his bony length and considered the chances of doing it. He was caught between two fires, and knew it. He gazed speculatively after the Kettle Creek men, moving off in a tight group now with Peterson at their head. Brophy's friends . . . And—to form the other arm of the pincers closing against him—Val Meeker and his Ladder gunmen.

Well, as Fox had said, the lockup was a tight-built little structure. If he could count on Peterson and the others, there would be a chance of holding off an attack should it come. Alone——He shrugged. It was all part of the game, chances he drew along with his seventy-five dollars a month. Yet a hard knot formed in his belly as he thought of his wife and the four girls.

But then he remembered one thing they had all seemed to let slip from their minds during the excitement of this last half hour. For there still was one of the Hardin brothers left. There was Clement.

2

Yes, there was Clem Hardin. And at that moment he was sitting on the lid of an oatbin at the stable, in hot shadows that made his face a dim, pale blob. The hands on his knees were clenched tight, and his voice had a tightness in it too.

"What am I gonna do, Limp?" he said for the third time.

Limp Kohler, the wrinkled little hostler, gave him a searching look. He set down a grain pail, shoved hands in the hip pockets of his worn bib overalls, and stood that way considering the boy.

He said finally: "Are you scared, Clem?"

"No," replied Clem slowly. "Not scared. Or maybe I am, but not just the way you mean. If I am, it's because I feel like the next move is up to me, and I don't know which way to turn."

"Yeah, I understand." The little man hobbled nearer in his warped and hesitant stride. "Tell me, kid," he said after a little silence. He put the question as though it were a hard one to ask. "You ain't broke up too much over what's happened to your brothers?"

Clem shook his head. "I should be, I reckon. But I don't seem to feel nothing except—it was a damn bad way to die! Jap and Noah never made it very easy for me to get real fond of them, you know. They was half-growed when Dad married a second time, and they resented it happening and they hated me soon as I was born—figured they'd have to cut me in someday on the ranch that they'd

12

got in the habit of thinking would be split two ways between them."

"I know. I remember when you was boys, the way they treated you. Old Sam used to switch 'em for it."

'Till the blood come," added Clem, nodding. "That didn't do no good—only made them hate me worse, I reckon. And though I'm big enough they've had to lay off me, it hasn't been any easier since Pop died—what with the way they've been running the Ladder."

Limp Kohler said, "This talk about Ladder ridin' last night and cuttin' fences—you hadn't no part of that, did you?"

The boy looked at him. "You know I didn't. I never knew what orders the crew was told to follow out."

"Just the same, folks in general are gonna be thinkin' now it's the same old Ladder, just another Hardin running it—and maybe one that's young enough he'll be easy for them to gang up on and lick. First they'll expect is for you to take it on yourself to do something about Nat Brophy, in return for him plugging your brothers. They're already looking for trouble from Meeker and the boys—and remember, as of right now, that tough crew is drawing your pay, nobody else's."

The knobby fists of the youngster on the oat box twitched a little and he put one of them up and pushed tawny hair back under the brim of the big hat he wore. His hand came away damp with sweat; Clem Hardin rubbed the knuckles thoughtfully across the front of his hickory shirt. He stood up then, slowly. "Thanks, Limp," he said, and his voice was tighter than ever. "I guess you've answered my question for me. You've showed me what I got to do."

The little cripple glanced at him anxiously. "You figure you'll be able to hold Meeker's crowd in line?"

"I dunno. I got to try. They're my responsibility, and

anything they might do would be square on my own head. I better get right out there to the ranch—should have started long ago."

He moved a little jerkily as he went to his sorrel gelding, turned the stirrup, and stepped up into saddle leather. The loosened shoe was tight now, and the horse was rested and ready for a run. Limp Kohler, hobbling after him, said, "You leaving town without a word with Bob Fox? You wouldn't want folks thinkin' you'd sneak out——"

"There isn't time," Clem told him shortly. "I got to be heading for Ladder."

The cripple let an arthritic claw of a hand rest on Clem's knee for an instant, and there was sympathy in his voice. "Good luck, boy." Then he stepped back and Clem rode past him, out of the hot shadows of the stable and into the hotter blast of the sun.

He avoided the main streets and left Tilden town unnoticed. He didn't want to see anyone, talk to anyone—not even Sally Fox. Clement Hardin had a job to do that promised to be a nasty one before he was through with it. And he knew no other way than to push ahead and tackle it straight on, before he might have a chance to lose his nerve.

So he let his sorrel out to a good pace and he held it at that as he went north across that rolling foothill range, following the dips and curves of the old wagon trail that threaded sage and buckbrush and lava outcropping. Not much of this land was fertile; it lay too close to the rock-ribbed hills, and too much of the thin soil had been lost in washouts and slides. The only real stretch of green was that which lay along Kettle Creek itself, and that stream was a wild one and cut a channel that had few points of access. Where the banks did level out enough for usefulness, the farmers had taken over. Except for those few spots, it was dry range fit only for cattle; but it had served Ladder well enough for a good many years.

Clem took the shallow crossing at Glenn's Ford, noting that even in this late season the waters of the creek, arising not many miles above him in the heart of the hills, had a rush and a current behind them that made a busy pattern of ripples over the stony shallows and broke cleanly against the hoofs of the sorrel as it plodded through. A gently cool, damp breath came funneling down the rocky channel, carried by the spray of the stream. It was curious to feel it against the cheek on a day that was otherwise so still and sultry.

The haze of the forest fire still hung against the sky, and it still added its irritating bite to the tang of road dust as he moved northward of the creek onto Hardin graze proper. That smoke haze was one of the inevitable signs of fall, though it was stronger in some years than in others. It all depended on the dryness of the season, the wind, the distance and spread of burning timber. It was too far away to worry about, of course, and the first rains would settle it. Meanwhile one soon got used to its acrid sting.

Presently Clem Hardin came in sight of buildings set at the foot of a rounded, brown, dry slope. It was bleak enough. Two women had had their try at softening the harshness of the low log ranch house, but that had been a long time ago and there were few signs remaining. After the death of his second wife, old Sam Hardin had let things run to hell. In Clement's memory it had always seemed a barren, ugly place, with its hand-hewn log buildings and the hard-packed dirt of the yard that was ungraced by any blade of grass.

A big windmill squealed as it swung its blades in what breeze came off the breadloaf hill behind the ranch. The corrals and outbuildings were serviceable, but that was all. There was no touch of beauty, and that Clem had always hated, a little vaguely. But it was his home; and now it was his ranch, and he was sole owner of the Ladder iron. This thought frightened him, although he as yet only half comprehended it.

All the way from town he had been aware that someone rode ahead of him; once he had caught brief sight of the man across the hills—a glimpse only, of the dark shape of horse and rider. But though Clem was in a hurry himself, he made no time on the man in front of him; and it occurred to him that there could be only one explanation for that. Somebody from town must be burning leather to warn Val Meeker and the Ladder crew about events there. Now, as Clem rode in under the high gateway and along the narrow wagon trail to the buildings, he saw a milling of men and horses in the yard and, even from a distance, could sense the excitement that gripped them.

He felt coldness knot up inside his belly. He thought of the loaded gun he carried in his saddle pocket, but he left it there. A gun wouldn't do him any good.

He sent his bronc into the dooryard of the main house and stepped down there, his legs feeling wooden under him and unlike any part of himself. So far no one seemed to have noticed his coming, except for Shorty, the cook, who stood alone at the kitchen door with a deep scowl on his homely, honest face. The activity was mainly yonder in front of the bunkhouse, where most of Ladder's crew were already mounted and others were leading horses from the corral, quickly piling on saddles and gear with grim and purposeful movements.

The center of interest appeared to be a dust-laden rider who did not belong on the pay roll. From the lathered look of his bronc, Clem knew this was the messenger from town even before he recognized him as a gambler who worked in Ed Pringle's dive, the Green Parrot. Pringle's was a favorite hangout for Meeker and the rest when they were in off the range, and Clem thought angrily that you could depend on him to stir up trouble if he could.

Now Val Meeker himself came striding from the bunkhouse, buckling on a belt and six-gun. He was a big man, possessed of a certain grace for all his bulk, and with powerful, lean hands whose smooth functioning fascinated Clem Hardin. His dark face with its roached black mustache was thunderous as he put his voice across the confusion of the yard: "Come on—mount up and we'll ride. We'll tear that damn town apart stick by stick, if we have to—but we'll get the skunk that did for Jap and Noah!"

Clement Hardin moved forward through the swirling dust. He had to try twice before he could lift his voice enough to be heard. "No! You're not riding anywhere!"

Slowly they came around to face him. Ladder had a big crew—nearly a dozen riders, all but two or three of them men who had come onto the range a year ago with Meeker, when Noah imported him to rod the Hardin ranch. There in front of them all, defying the frenzy of anger that the killings had built in them, Clem felt suddenly very much alone.

And now Val Meeker moved toward him, striding with a pantherish grace. There was a promise of leashed danger in him, always. He halted six feet from Clem and he said into a sudden hush: "Did you remark something?"

The youngster had to fight down a sick terror as he looked across at the other. He had the makings of a big man, did Clement Hardin, but he hadn't filled out yet to keep up with his weedlike growth. And tall as he was, he had to tilt his tawny head up a little to challenge Val Meeker's black, hard stare.

This was just as bad as he had known it would be. Yet

doggedly he pushed ahead with it. He said. "You're not any of you ridin' to town. That's an order—a Hardin order! And as long as you're on the Ladder pay roll it's my orders now you'll have to take!"

"Why, you pup!" Scorn quirked the foreman's lips. "You mean you're calling yourself by a man's name? And you without even the guts to see your brothers' killer get what he has coming to him?"

"Nat Brophy is in the law's hands. The law will settle with him."

"Maybe," said Val Meeker. "But on the other hand, maybe we don't aim to let it. The Hardins—the *real* Hardins—were men; we ain't just standin' around doin' nothin' while we wait for some judge to make up his mind. And we ain't lettin' ourselves be stopped by a spineless, yella——"

Clem hit him. He did it desperately, knowing it was what Meeker wanted and had been building to. The big, raw-knuckled fist splatted against the side of Meeker's tough jaw, and the gunman fell back a little but quickly caught himself. Someone yelled, fell instantly silent. The two stood there facing each other a moment.

Blood had rushed into the foreman's face, and the marks of Clem's knuckles were plain against it. Now, slowly, Val Meeker dropped both hands down to the gun belt that snugged against his lean waist. Clement Hardin, himself unarmed, felt a quick leap of panic—but Meeker did not draw. Instead he unhooked the buckle with the quick jerk of his hand and, taking off the gun and belt, flung them to one side. One of his men caught it; he didn't look to see, his black eyes burning all the time sharply and unblinking at Clem.

"You're gonna be sorry you did that!" he said softly. "Believe me, you are. Much as I hate to waste the time it'll take to work you over!"

Clem waited, unmoving. And then Meeker came in with a smashing blow that drove the slighter man stumbling backward.

He would hardly have thought, the ease with which it started across, that the fist could have had such power behind it. Dazed, he caught himself, had to wait a minute before he could retaliate; but Val Meeker didn't let him have that minute.

The foreman waded in after his first blow, arms pistoning. Clem Hardin backpedaled, trying desperately to build up some kind of defense. He got across a right that landed against Meeker's hard mouth; he felt the sharp pain of a tooth against his knuckle and there was blood starting from Meeker's lip a moment later. But it didn't stop the man, and that was the most effective blow the Hardin youngster managed to put over.

Fists rocked his head, blurred his vision. All at once a boot heel caught on something and he went down, despite his efforts to stay erect. Dust billowed chokingly. Through it he saw Meeker coming straight in to use his boots, and he rolled just in time to avoid them.

He heard the shouts that had gone up from the crew when they thought Meeker had the fight ended. And he sensed, in that dizzy moment as he cleared the kick that swung at him, and got his knees and then his feet under him, that all this hardcase Ladder crew despised and hated him. Like his brothers, they had tolerated him because he was only a youngster, and because he had kept quietly out of the way. But now he was daring to set himself up in the place of a man, and asserting his authority as the new owner of Ladder ranch. For this presumption he must be punished.

Bitterness was in him, and a vast loneliness.

Then Val Meeker was coming at him again. He did not retreat. A dogged, stubborn pride made him stand where he was and swing recklessly into his opponent. He would show this tough outfit who was a man and who wasn't, or he would go down beaten. . . .

He went down. He hadn't a chance against the solid, compact strength of the gunman. He went down with a blow crashing square into his face, and this time when he hit the earth he failed to clear the swing of the foreman's cowhide boot. It landed heavily, knocking the wind from him. He thought in dull pain that it might have caved a rib too. But he could only lie there, numb and gasping, and sorely beaten.

Val Meeker stood above him, panting a little, dark face twisted with the lust of hurting. He lifted the back of a hand to his cut lip and looked briefly at the blood, and then he told the half-conscious form in the dust: "I'm through with this ranch! I wouldn't be connected with it now. But we all of us got three weeks' pay coming and we'll be back later to collect—don't think we won't."

He heeled away, with a gesture for his watching men. "All right—hit the saddle for town!"

Someone handed him his six-gun and he strapped it in place about his flat hips, strode to where his black was saddled and waiting. Most of the crew was already mounted. One held the reins for his chief.

Clement Hardin climbed slowly to his feet, sobbing to drag air into tortured lungs. The lot of them were ignoring him now. He looked about quickly, saw the cook coming at a run from the chuck shack, saw his own sorrel gelding on trailing reins where he had left it, only a few yards away. He went to it, stumbling. He fumbled into the saddle pocket and found the loaded six-gun, brought it out.

When he tried to yell at the men his voice failed him. Val Meeker was in saddle now, kneeing his bronc out to the front of the group of milling horses. He had to get their attention some way . . . Clem Hardin poked his gun muzzle into the air and pulled the trigger blindly.

It brought their heads around, their stares spearing him. And standing there on spread legs, wobbly, with blood on his battered face and the tawny hair spilling down into his bleared eyes, the youngster shouted hoarsely: "The next shot empties a saddle! Now, the lot of you pile out of leather—hear me? You're leaving Brophy and that jail alone!"

"Why, damn you!" grunted Val Meeker, on a tone of exasperation. He must have seen, however, that Clem Hardin was driving himself on nerve alone and that the hand with that heavy weapon weighting it had little strength to aim and fire. At any rate, he dared a sudden move for his own belted gun despite the muzzle that was pointed at him.

He never had to pull it. For next instant Clem Hardin crumpled slowly, went down senseless upon his face. The gun spilled out of his hand as he fell. He lay there without moving, and Meeker stabbed his half-drawn gun back into holster. "Out cold!" he muttered. And lifting the reins, with a jerk of his head toward the Tilden trail: "Come on, buckos—let's ride!"

3

A FARMER named Luke Sands brought word of Val Meeker's coming. He dragged his big work-horse steed to a dust-plunging halt in front of the jail, raising a shout that echoed all along the false-fronted line of buildings, and fetched Bob Fox and Tom Peterson hurrying out of the marshal's office. "Got the whole Ladder crew with him," Sands announced in a high-pitched, scared voice. "Eight or nine of them. They just pulled into that Green Parrot dive at the edge of town, and they were talking loud about taking this jail apart log by log and stringing Nat Brophy to the nearest cottonwood!"

"You say they stopped at Pringle's?" Tom Peterson echoed. He exchanged looks with the marshal. "Likkerin' up first! Maybe they'll go and get themselves too blind drunk to shoot straight——"

Bob Fox shook his head morosely; there was a knot beginning to tighten in his belly. "Not that crowd! Maybe, if they was only ordinary cowhandlers; but they ain't that. They're tough—and booze will just make them harder to cope with." He shrugged gaunt shoulders. "Still and all, the delay should give us a little chance to be ready for them. Tom, go round up your friends and get them here —pronto. *With* their guns!"

"Sure!" But the granger leader had a dubious look as he started away at a half run. Perhaps he wasn't downright sure how many of the Kettle Creek farmers he could count on, now that the issue was actually about to be joined.

Bob looked around quickly. A couple of saddle horses lazed near by at tie racks, and he said, "Luke, better move those broncs. Take them somewhere else and tie them where they won't be apt to collect flying bullets." He added sharply: "And when you've done it, be sure and come back!"

He added that because Luke Sands was looking a bit green around the mouth. Apparently he was too excited even to notice the barb in the lawman's warning; pulling away, he yanked reins too hard and the big rawboned sorrel under him started to buck in protest. Then Luke Sands had him straightened out and was leaning from saddle to jerk loose the knots anchoring the tied horses.

Bob Fox watched him ride off, leading them. The marshal was wondering a little about himself. What he ought to do, he supposed, was head straight for the Green Parrot and catch Meeker there—have the thing out face to face, and not give the Ladder tough crew a chance to likker up and bring their guns shooting into the town proper. Maybe a firm stand now could ward off violence and bloodshed. . . . He saw the logic of that. But he also saw the danger, and he knew himself well enough to know he wasn't going to act on the idea.

Nine to one seemed like awfully long odds. And pinning a marshal's badge on a man's shirt front didn't turn him overnight into a hero—nor yet into a complete idiot, who would try to talk down a whirlwind and send it somewhere else to strike.

So instead he turned and strode back into the jail, where Nat Brophy stood clutching the bars of his cell with the sweat streaming on his face—sweat not caused entirely by the stuffy heat of the little crackerbox building. "I heard you talking!" Brophy cried hoarsely. "They're coming for me! But you got to keep the promise you made! You got to protect your prisoner, Marshal!"

"Oh, shut up!" growled Bob Fox wearily.

He got a rifle down from its pegs and checked the action and the loading with methodical movements; outwardly he seemed calm enough, his solemn, bony face showing none of the anxiety with which he considered the problem in front of him.

Tilden's jail was a small, compact structure of thick and solid log sidings, a partition dividing the front office from the two cells in the rear. Each cell contained a small barred window, high up; there were two windows in the office, one in the front wall near the thick door, another at one side over the battered desk and caboose chair. Store buildings enclosed the jail to north and south, but the rear lay open—nothing back there but a vacant lot choked with weeds.

All in all, it seemed hard to believe that a lynch mob, however numerous, could do much against a resolute defending force that wasn't afraid to stand up to their bullets.

Luke Sands came back from his mission with the horses; he was a short, stocky man, a bachelor, in his forties and running some to baldness. Right now he was scared pretty close to panic, but he had come back, and Bob Fox was grateful for any help. Sands had no long gun—only the wooden-handled revolver stuffed into the waistband of his jeans. Fox said, "Get that shotgun leaning in the corner. It's loaded with washers and scrap iron and it will tear a hole in the side of a barn."

The granger picked up the weapon gingerly and brought it to the dusty front window, where Bob Fox was leaning on his rifle and peering out into the silent street. No life showed there. It was the golden hour when sunlight put long slants through dust-laden air. Luke Sands said nervously, "How long is Meeker going to hold off?"

"How would I know?" the marshal grunted, irked by the senseless question. "He might not come at all."

"You really think so, maybe?" The momentary false hopefulness was gone from his voice a moment later as Sands exclaimed: "Hey, here's Peterson back—but he's alone!"

The Swede had acquired a couple of rifles somewhere and he carried one under each arm. His red face looked thoroughly angry; when Fox swung open the heavy door for him, Peterson clumped in and dropped the weapons in a clatter onto the desk, and he didn't seem able for a moment to meet the marshal's dour glance. "Well?" said Fox. "Where are your friends?"

"About half of 'em went home!" Tom Peterson blurted. "Those dirty, yellow-bellied——"

"All right. What about the other half?"

Peterson shrugged meaty shoulders. "Some of them said they'd be along directly. They had to dig up guns." He shook his head, mouth twisting on sour words. "But them others! All the big talk they make, and then when you need 'em to back your play——"

"I could have told you," Bob Fox said without rancor. "That's people. That's what you got to deal with."

Back in his cell, Nat Brophy was putting up another fuss. "You're gonna give me a gun, ain't you? You're gonna at least let me put up a fight for my life when those killers come? You *got* to——"

"Aw, go to hell!" Peterson growled at him in high disgust.

Time ran out with seemingly unbearable slowness. The prisoner in the cell, and the three men in the jail office, waited out endless dragging moments; and nothing happened. Not even the deliberate ticking of a clock marked the passing of that golden hour before sunset. As yet no recruits had come to swell their narrow ranks. Out on the street, no life stirred. Bob Fox kept his eye on the north end of it, for from there, he knew, would come first warning of the Ladder crew's approach.

Suddenly he was a little shocked to see his eldest daughter hurrying along the walk toward the jail.

She moved purposefully, her chin up, a long-legged stride bringing her straight in on that spot where danger threatened—she had inherited something from her father and for a girl was rather above the average in height. With a grunt of anger Bob Fox heeled and strode quickly to the door, stepped out carrying his rifle. He met his daughter in front of the jail and said: "Darn it, what are you doing here? Ain't you got any fool sense?"

She faced him squarely, her head up, the sun finding little glints of gold in her brushed-back brown curls. She had good features, a strong chin that was just rounded enough to keep it from being blunt, brown eyes like her dad's. Bob worshiped her with a love that the coming of three other daughters had done nothing to lessen.

Sally Fox said, "What's happened to *your* fool sense? You're going to get yourself killed before this is finished!" There was maybe a sign of tears in her eyes, though Sally never cried. "Don't go through with it, Pop!"

He shrugged gaunt shoulders. "What would you have me do, girl? I got a job."

"But this isn't any part of it! You're a town officer; this range squabble doesn't concern you. Put Nat Brophy on a fast horse and turn him loose, and Meeker and the rest will set after him and leave the town in peace."

The marshal looked at his daughter reprovingly. "Why, Sally! That don't sound like you! Are you forgetting Nat Brophy committed murder—right here in my town? That being true, I have to hold him for the sheriff. And it means I have to protect him too; with my life, if necessary." He added heavily, "I'm no great shucks as a lawman, but at least I hope I know my duty and ain't afraid to stick to it."

The girl bit her lower lip, looked away from him. A yellow-headed cottonwood shook its leaves above the squat jail, and she fixed her eyes on that as she said slowly, "I'm sorry, Pop. I didn't think. Just selfish, I guess—I don't want to lose you to no tin marshal's badge . . ."

His face softened. "I know, Sally."

"Pop!" She looked back at him suddenly, a hidden distress flooding her face. "Pop, what do you suppose they've done to Clem?"

"What do you mean?"

"I was just talking to Limp Kohler; he says Clem was in town this morning, the time of the shooting. He headed back to Ladder right away, to try and keep Meeker and the rest of them in line. But—you can see, something must have happened!"

Her own distress was mirrored in her father's eyes, hearing this, but he tried quickly to cover up, to dissemble. "The boy's got a head on him," Bob said gruffly. "I can't think he'd walk right into trouble against a crew that size." But he sounded unconvincing, and he knew it. And the only effect of his speech was to increase the unhappiness in his daughter's look and make her lip tremble a little.

The marshal frowned. "You're really pretty much concerned about young Hardin, ain't you? You like him pretty well?" She dropped her eyes, nodded miserably. Old Bob put a gentle hand on her arm. "Look, girl! We don't *know* anything has happened. Now, you better get on home to your mother and the kids. You ain't doing any good here."

"But I want to help!"

"Sure you do," he agreed. "And the best help you can give me now is to stay with your mother, so I'll know she ain't all alone in this hour and has got you there to lean on. You'll do that for me, won't you?"

"Of course, Pop."

"And don't worry too much about—anything. It don't solve any problems."

He stood in the hot sunshine and watched her go, something of the stiffness missing now from the set of her shoulders. *Clem Hardin,* he thought. He turned quickly, shot a scowling look upstreet toward the dark doorway of the saloon. Sally was right, of course; something must have happened to Clem, and the thought made anger start boiling in Bob Fox as nothing else that had so far happened. Damn it, he liked that boy!

He dragged air into his lungs, and the sting of smoke in it made him cough a time or two. Over at the tobacco shop he saw the old proprietor in the doorway, watching him. Otherwise it was really amazing how empty a town could become all of a sudden—and how taut with a silent waiting . . .

Two of the nesters came along the sidewalk, toting rifles awkwardly. They looked frightened, but with a kind of determination in them. "Where do you want us, Marshal?"

Fox thought quickly. "Peterson and Sands are in the office, with me. You boys take that empty store across the street. We'll get 'em from two directions that way, and if they want gunplay they can have it. Yeah, that's the best plan."

They nodded and moved at a run across the street dust, trailing their guns. Five men, Fox thought. Five men to hold off a small army . . . He went back into the jail office, to hear Nat Brophy's continued whining beyond the bars of the cell.

Peterson said, "He wants out."

"Better off where he is," Fox grunted.

The red-faced Swede said heavily, "If he don't close his whining mouth, I'll personally close it for him in a minute!"

"Beginning to wish you hadn't thrown your weight on his oar?" the marshal suggested dryly, looking at him. Peterson scowled.

"I didn't say that," he muttered. "I told you before, I'm seeing Nat Brophy through this. And you ain't hangin' him, either!" he added belligerently.

The old man didn't bridle. He only said, "Don't reckon I am. That's a job for the sheriff——"

Then, even before Luke Sands finished a startled outcry, he was whirling toward the door as the scud of nearing hoofs laid a growing pulsation across the stillness. He stepped outside, rifle butt pressed at the ready against one gaunt hip, the weapon steady in his bony hands. And there came Val Meeker and the Ladder toughs.

They came at a dead run, and they came shooting; the pop of guns started when they were still blocks away, when the men and mounts made only a dark, shifting pattern behind the sun-gilded dust haze filling the street from wall to wall. The way they wasted ammunition, Bob Fox knew the lot of them were drunk, but that didn't necessarily mean they would be any the less dangerous. Just nasty-mean, maybe, and honing to spill blood.

And as the hoof sound swelled to pulsing thunder in the street, the bunch of them burst suddenly into view through the dust curtain and came sweeping straight down on the squat structure of the jail. Bob had already given his men orders, but he called again to them in a taut voice, "Hold fire! I'll start any shooting!" He didn't know whether they could hear him or not.

He lifted the rifle, set its butt into the hollow of his

shoulder, and brought his sights into alignment on Val
Meeker's wide chest, spotting the leader easily at the head
of his gang. He held the bead, the black muzzle of the
long gun unwavering as the riders came whirling in. A
shouted warning would not have stopped them, but the
gun did it; the Ladder foreman wavered visibly, and suddenly he was hauling rein, cursing as he flung up a hand
to halt the men behind him.

Fear and fury were mingled in his dark face. The way
he kept his balance uncertainly in the saddle hinted at
the amount of liquor he must have consumed at Pringle's.
They were all drunk strictly. And just to that degree the
more dangerous.

"Put that gun down, you old fool!" Val Meeker roared.
"You ain't the man who can buck us."

"I can sure as hell pick *you* out of leather, though,"
Bob Fox answered him, and there was nothing mild about
him right then. "Want to come ahead and let me try it?"

Indecision laid its mark on the big man then. He wasn't
too drunk to see his danger, and he sat there on a fidgety
bronc with one hand tight on the reins, a smoking gun
filling the other, and gnawed at one end of his roached
mustache. The tension stretched out and became a fragile
thing that a word or a sudden movement could shatter.
And Bob's arms were getting shaky, holding a bead that
long. The sights began to wobble across Meeker's red-
checked shirt.

Alarmed at this, he cried hoarsely, "I'm countin' to
three——"

Maybe Meeker sensed what was happening to the marshal. Maybe a grunted word or a signal passed between
him and the rider at his left hand. In any event, he suddenly was wrenching his body sharply to one side at the
same instant that his companion swung and threw a hasty
shot at the old man with the rifle.

The bullet missed, narrowly, peeling a splinter from the door's edge behind Bob. His own finger cramped trigger, but he knew he was flinching and that his shot wasn't any good. Being only a normally brave man, then, the marshal was stumbling backward, throwing himself frantically toward the haven of the open door as general shooting began and built to a quick crescendo of gun racket.

From the jail and from the empty store across the street's dusty confusion, Fox's men threw their shots into the ruck of milling horses and yelling shouting men. The voices of the guns slapped against false fronts, mounting on swirling dust toward the sunset colors in the sky overhead. The *br-room* of Luke Sand's shotgun bellowed above the other sounds. A horse screamed its mortal pain, went down heavily as its rider leaped clear.

Caught in a cross fire, and with no decent target for their own lead, the Ladder crew couldn't hold very long. Suddenly they broke and scattered, pulling back from the unequal battle. One reached a hand to the man who had lost his bronc, swept him up behind saddle, and took him along that way. Another was doubled over, gripping a broken arm. Otherwise none of the raiders seemed to have been much hurt in the wild melee of gunfire, and Bob Fox, lowering his smoking rifle, turned aside from the doorway to check quickly on his companions.

Peterson had a cut on one cheek that was bleeding, but it had been made not by a bullet but by a flying shard of glass as the window above his head went out. Neither Bob nor Luke Sands had been touched, and he hoped the same was true of the pair he had posted across the street—a stratagem which touched him with a moment's pride now as he realized how well it had worked out. Back in his cell, Nat Brophy was making incoherent babbling noises, caught tight in the grip of horror; but no bullet had penetrated that far into the little jail.

The face of Luke Sands was beaded in sweat and sickly white with fear. He scraped a hand across wet jowls. "That—that was bad, for a minute."

"We ain't through yet," grunted Peterson. He had smeared a sleeve through the bloody scratch on his cheek and was now methodically feeding a new clip into his rifle's smoking chamber. Bob Fox slanted an anxious look upstreet, from the doorway. A half block away Meeker had pulled his forces together, and already they were turning, bunching——

"Watch it!"

They were coming again, with an insane persistence; once again the guns built up their thunder. The tough crew streamed past the jail in a shuttling of horses and swirl of dust, guns popping. Then suddenly, above the other racket, Fox heard Nat Brophy screaming frenziedly for help.

He whirled toward the strap-iron cell door and, through the grating, saw Brophy down on his knees in a corner, trying to cram his body into a narrow space out of line from the window in the rear wall. For out there was movement!

Briefly a stubble-bearded face showed beyond the bars, a man leaning from saddle to peer into the cell shadows. A gun muzzle poked through, slanting toward the prisoner crouching in the corner. In the instant before Bob could get his hot-barreled rifle up and put a hasty shot through the door grille, the six-gun drove a ribbon of fire and smoke into the cell.

The shot missed, but neither did Bob's shell have any effect. You couldn't shoot effectively at that angle, and there wasn't time to get the key from the desk and unlock the door.

Bob Fox did a reckless thing then. He turned and bolted at a run from the office, his long legs scissoring. Without regard for the near whine of lead, he sprinted along the front of the jail, rounded the corner, kept going. He saw that a pair of riders were back there, having come down the alley under cover of the main frontal attack; they were crowding each other at the window, trying to find Brophy and direct a six-gun slug at him. Bob dropped one of these in a sprawl from saddle, went to one knee while he worked the lever and lifted the rifle stock to his cheek. His next shot met the flame of the second rider's gun . . .

And then, as abruptly as they struck, the raiders were going. With a final spatter of bullets they drummed away on down the street, strung out, whooping and yelling. They went out of Tilden town like that, and slowly the silence threaded back. The dust settled and the smoke lifted; the cottonwood's leaves twinkled again in the sun. Now, all over town, doors were slamming, voices yelling as running men began converging on the jail.

Tom Peterson showed in the doorway, lugging a smoking rifle; he yelled, "Bob! Bob Fox!" Not hearing an answer, he started at a hasty run toward the alley; a moment later his cry of horror was bringing others to join him, there in back of the jail.

For the marshal was down, in a growing welter of blood, and not far from the sprawled shape of the raider he had killed. He was not dead, however, but dazed with bullet shock. "My leg!" he groaned, stirring. "They skewered it!"

"Let me see."

Peterson squatted and reached to touch the gaunt, red-soaked leg, but Fox struck his hand aside. "Get away, damn it! Fetch me a doctor. I'm bleedin' like a stuck pig —maybe an artery, for all I know."

"Doc Warn's legging it up the street now," Luke Sands reported.

Peterson said, "Does it hurt, Bob?"

"Hell yes, it hurts!" the marshal gritted between set teeth. "They get anybody else? How's Brophy?"

"Yelling too loud to have anything the matter with him——"

Luke Sands looked a little green now that the thing was over. "What do you think? Will they be back?"

"I'm no mind reader," Bob Fox growled tightly. "But if they do, it will be to finish the job."

He thought, grinning against the pain of his hurt leg, *And what am I going to do then?*

4

THEY carried the marshal the half block to his house, after Doc Warn had applied a tourniquet to stop the copious bleeding. Mrs. Fox saw them coming and had water heating on the wood range, the smaller children shooed out from underfoot, and a place ready to stretch the hurt man out on his own bed. Bob Fox lay there twisting, his face white as the pillow from pain and loss of blood. "Damn it!" he said. "I got a prisoner in the jail, Doc! I can't lie here like this."

"You can and you will," the doctor said as he shrugged out of his coat and began rolling up his shirt sleeves. "That bullet nicked an artery, don't you understand? Now, lie still and let me work!"

Tom Peterson said, "Luke and I will get back to the jail. We'll stand guard."

"Just a minute, Tom!" snapped the marshal in a voice that made the blond nester turn back to face him. "Just so's you won't go plowing through everything in the office, the key to Brophy's cell is in the upper right-hand drawer of the desk. But—if anybody should use that key to set Brophy loose while I'm not there to prevent it, I'll have to hold you personally responsible, understand? I'm sorry," he added, seeing the flush of anger that spread up through Peterson's face. "I'm sorry, Pete, but I had to warn you!"

The granger opened his mouth, closed it again, as though stunned beyond speech. Then, without answering, he heeled around, gave Luke Sands a jerk of the head. The two farmers tramped out.

"Bob!" the marshal's tired-faced wife exclaimed. "Should you have talked like that, when they offered to help?"

"They ain't helping me," he answered tightly. "They're looking out for their friend Brophy. Maybeso I'm as well off to be laid up awhile. If Val Meeker comes again, I got a notion just to lie here and let 'em have the jail to fight their war out between them. . . . Where's my pipe?"

Sally fetched it, filled it with rough-cut, held a match while he sucked its flame down into the charred bowl. "Good girl," he grunted approvingly, smiling up at her through the first puffs of smoke. He lay with shoulders propped against the pillow, smoking and watching critically while the doctor worked on his hurt leg." "A clean cut, Doc?" he said.

"Yes," said Warn. "Deep, but clean. The bullet went right through."

Sweat stood on the marshal's bloodless face. His wife came and wiped his forehead tenderly with a damp cloth; when he looked at her he saw the tears in her eyes.

"Don't worry, Maw," he said. "Everything's all right. I'll be up and around in a day or two, and the council won't take my job just because of this. You and the girls'll be all right."

"Oh, Bob!" She was weeping now. "If it wasn't for me and the girls, you wouldn't have to take such chances! You're not a young man any more; it ain't worth the risk, or what they pay you. Seventy-five a month! Just because of us——"

"Tut-tut, Maw!" He got her worn hand, held it in both of his. "You know life wouldn't be anything without my womenfolks."

They clung together, two aging people, and pain worked in the lips that were clamped around Bob Fox's pipe as Doc Warn did his job methodically, without any comment.

Sally Fox went out onto the back stoop and stood there a moment, letting what breeze there was touch her and looking at the long golden light of the westering sun as it laid its shadows across the bare dirt yard. She felt suddenly shaky in the joints, and recognized this as an aftermath of the terror that had seized her when the first volley of shooting had ripped across the town's quiet.

Now the real danger was over; her father had been hit, but not too badly, and the doctor was there to patch him whole again. And now, when there was no point to it, the panic hit her with a flutter of the heart that constricted her labored breathing; she leaned against the doorframe, a hand pressed to her breast, fighting the quick nausea of reaction.

As it passed, another fear that had been pushed aside by the excitement of the last hour flooded in on her again —returned all the stronger for having been, for the moment, forgotten. Suddenly she knew that she could not go on in this uncertainty.

Just then her three sisters came running out of the chicken house. The youngest was crying, and all three were white and scared. "Pop's all right," Sally told them patiently. "Vingie, you get inside and see if there's anything you can do to help Maw. You other kids stay here, out of the way."

"Where are you going?" Vingie, the next oldest, demanded.

"Something I just got to do," Sally answered briefly. But she had to delay long enough to blow the baby's nose for her, wipe the tears from her grimy face. "You mustn't cry, Beth," she said soothingly. "There's nothing to cry about now——" But when the wailing increased, Sally straightened with a sigh, pushed Beth toward Agnes, the fourth girl. "Do something to amuse her," she ordered. "I just can't wait around . . ."

She went in her quick, long-legged stride toward the livery barn; she walked like a boy, and looked very much like one in her bib overalls and much-laundered shirt. "Limp!" she exclaimed breathlessly as she met the old cripple in the wide doorway. "Is the buckskin handy? Can I take her?"

The man looked at her shrewdly and nodded. "Right in that end stall," said Limp, pointing an arthritic finger.

Sally had no horse of her own, but by a secret agreement with Limp, the old hostler loaned her a stable bronc free of charge whenever she needed one. As she moved quickly now, taking blanket, saddle, gear off the pegs and piling them on the fast little buckskin mare, Limp stood watching with a speculative look in his faded eyes. "How's your paw?" he demanded.

"He'll be all right. Got it in the leg." She stood with boots braced wide apart, giving the latigo a jerk to draw the girths in tight. "Doc says not to worry."

"That's good." Limp scratched his stubbled jaw, said nothing more until Sally swung up into the saddle and pulled the buckskin's head around toward the door. Then he called after her, just as she kicked the smooth flank with a spurless heel: "Look out you don't run into Meeker's gang, twixt here and Ladder."

Now, how did he know that's where I was riding? she wondered. Certain sure, not much escaped crippled old Limp Kohler. . . .

The low sunlight hit her, and moments later she was out of town with the twin ribbons of the wagon road ahead; and here she let the pony out. After all the waiting, she had a feeling suddenly that she was racing against time. The little mare felt like a run. Sally let it go until the first spurt was out, and then she had control of her own emotions and she curbed the horse gently, drew it down to an easier pace. It was too great a distance to let the buckskin wear itself out that way.

She raised no sign of Meeker's gang. She wondered where they had headed after that brief skirmish at the jail. Maybe they would leave Kettle Creek Range now, make one less wearing problem for its people to face . . . But she didn't really put much hope in that. Val Meeker and his whole crew had been imported by Jap and Noah Hardin at gun wages, and they wouldn't be apt to pull out so soon, empty-handed, just because the Hardins were dead now. Not a crew of Meeker's stripe.

Sally was wise in such matters. She wasn't the daughter of a lawman for nothing.

But, at any rate, Meeker didn't seem to have returned to Ladder. All was quiet there as she came in on the ranch buildings at the foot of the sugarloaf. Only a couple of horses in the corral, and no one in the yard. Sally kicked her pony, rode the last quarter mile with a lump of fear in her throat again. It was sunset, and the smoke haze over the western hills made the light reddish and dull as the sun dropped lower into it.

Then she was dragging rein in front of the big log ranch house, and as she did so Clem Hardin opened the door and came out. He stood there in the last light, not making any move or giving a greeting.

"Clem!"

The surge of relief that went through her at sight of him quickly changed to something else. Sally swung down lightly, running forward to meet him. "Oh, Clem!" His face, she saw now, was a puffed and swollen mass of bruises, with one eye closed and the brow above it torn and ragged. When he tried to smile at her a split lip made his mouth twist painfully.

"Hello, Sally," he muttered.

"Clem! What—what happened?"

He shrugged. "I tried to play a man's part; I reckon I got learned!" He put up a hand in a characteristic gesture, to paw unruly yellow hair out of his eyes. She caught the wince he made as he said, "That was a part of it—a cowhide boot with a foot inside! Shorty Jones taped me up. Can't tell if a rib was splintered or not."

Tears stung her eyes and she blinked against them. "It was Meeker's bunch? You tried to keep them out of Tilden and they piled you?"

"No," he said, shaking his head disgustedly. "It took only one man to do this. I talked big and tough, and Val Meeker just naturally tore me apart, singlehanded. What I get for trying to pass myself off for full-growed!" He shrugged. "But it don't matter what happened to me——"

"It does too, Clem!"

He wouldn't listen to her. The aftermath of his beating, the weariness it had put all through his tired and muscle-sore body, had filled him with a feeling of self-loathing. "I take it Meeker went to Tilden, all right," he grunted. "Tell me what happened, Sally. I want to know."

"It was pretty bad, Clem . . ." They sat together on the doorsill and she told him hurriedly of the raid and of the wounding of her father. For a long time they talked, while the high smoke pall across the dying sun put lurid reddish light across the land, and then the shadows poured in. Clement Hardin's face turned grimmer in the growing dusk. He didn't hear the first time when Shorty Jones came to tell them that stew was on the table and coffee ready to pour.

"I don't want anything to eat," he grunted.

"Whatta you mean, you don't want nothin' to eat?" cried Shorty, bridling. "Listen, I'm the only man on your crew that ain't quit you, but nothing says I can't draw my time, too, if you're gonna start turning down perfectly good grub after all the trouble I've gone to fixin' it." The little cook turned to Sally. "You better reason with him, Miss Sally. He's gone and got me too riled for arguin'."

"Food will do you good, Clem," Sally said. "And it's only fair to Shorty. Come on—please!"

Clem would have sworn he wasn't able to choke down any kind of food, but the aroma from the steaming dishes on the cookshack table changed his mind for him. Shorty was one good cow-camp cook. He watched over the boy and girl while they ate, and kept their plates loaded with beef stew and biscuits and their coffee cups filled, and his wizened face was wrinkled in deep concern as he watched Clem and listened to him talk.

"I got to do something!" Clement Hardin said tightly. "So far I've only made a fool of myself. But it's up to me to stop Meeker somehow."

"But why?" insisted Sally. "He's off your pay roll now. "It's no longer your responsibility what he and his riders do."

"You think not? Hardins brought them in on this range—and I'm a Hardin. That makes it my responsibility. What's more, Ladder has always been the big iron on Kettle Creek. If it don't take a stand now, any respect it's ever built for itself hereabouts goes down the drain. For Dad's sake, I can't afford to let that happen. That's why I got to do something."

A heavy silence fell over the cookshack as he went on eating, shoveling the meat and potatoes into him, his tawny hair gleaming like dry straw in the lamplight. Off in the hills somewhere the yapping of a coyote floated down on the beginning of a night breeze that came across the land loaded with pine scent and the tang of a distant fire burning itself out somewhere off in the forested peaks.

Sally only toyed with her own food, trying to think of words that would help Clem in this hour of hard decision. It occurred to her suddenly that nothing at all had been said about the death of his two half brothers, and when she tried belatedly to frame some appropriate sentiment she realized that it would ring false and left it unspoken. She doubted greatly that there was any real grief in Clem over the loss of Jap and Noah. They had not been like real brothers at all—not ever. They had inherited from old Sam Hardin a streak of meanness that had never showed up in this towheaded, unhappy youngster across the table from her.

"Got some pipin'-hot dried-apple pie here." Shorty spoke up quickly as Clem suddenly put down knife and fork, pushed back his chair.

"Later, Shorty," said Clem. He stood up, got his hat from the back of the chair, and went out into the night. At once Sally was after him, remembering to pause long enough to thank Shorty for the grub. The little cook nodded sourly.

"Better keep an eye on him," he grunted, jerking his head toward the door. "He's up to something."

"I will, Shorty."

At the corral she found Clem tightening the cinches on his sorrel horse. When she heard his grunt of pain, saw how gingerly he worked so as to favor his hurt side, she took the latigo from his hand and jerked up the girths herself, not looking at him in the dusk as she said, "Where are you riding, Clem?"

"To town."

"Not looking for Val Meeker?" she said in a muffled voice. "All by yourself?"

He told her, "There's something I just remembered, Sally. When they rode out of here, Mart Raines was forking a Ladder-branded horse—a chestnut bay. It belongs to me—and no matter what, I can't let them walk off with Ladder saddle stock. I got to go after that bronc and get it back!"

"But—but why not send word to the sheriff, at Maxwell? Horse stealing is something the law should handle."

"Can't you understand? This is my job to do! A Hardin has always seen fit to stomp his own snakes. I guess you think I ain't man enough—well, maybe I ain't. But sure to God I can make a try!" His voice was bitter.

Sally's hand went to his arm, tightened on the sleeve of the shirt. "No, Clem! No! I don't think any such a thing about you! I guess—I guess you ought to know what I think, to have ridden out here the way I did this afternoon——"

They stood close together in the gray darkness, just a boy and a girl who had both seen bad trouble since the coming up of the sun that morning. Sally Fox knew an aching in her breast, a melting feeling of pity for Clem that was mingled with something more. Surely he wasn't deaf, or blind—or too dumb, either, to understand what she was trying to tell him. She couldn't put it any plainer and be a lady.

Why couldn't he slip his arm around her just once, the way she had been dreaming he would for years now—in fact, since she was old enough to have such dreams at all? For just a moment, as she stood there with her face tilted up to his and the night breeze touching them, she thought it was going to happen——

Then, abruptly, Clem Hardin turned away from her. He put a hand on the skirt of his saddle, smoothed it down. "Get your horse," he said. "I'll ride back to town with you."

"All right, Clem."

Probably he was too wrought up to notice how he had hurt her.

5

SHE asked as they rode across the range southward: "Do you have any ideas where to go looking for Meeker?"

"One or two," Clem told her shortly, and that was as much as he would talk about it. Silence settled over them, silence broken only by the clink of bit chains, the creak of saddle leather, the thud of their horses' hoofs on the dark ground. Though she rode stirrup to stirrup with Clem, Sally had never felt farther away from him.

A white moon came up and laid its silver wash of light across the rolling sage. The mountains shouldered against the sky, like flat cutouts of black cardboard pasted there. A chill came in, reminding them that, despite the heat of the day just past, this was really the season of frosts and of the first cold rains.

Twenty minutes passed. They were nearing Kettle Creek when Sally suddenly reined in close to Clem. "Did you hear gunfire just then? Like a gust of wind carried it——"

He hauled in, frowning at the night as he listened. "I don't——" he began, and then another breath of breeze fanning across the dark land brought a louder rattle of shots. "It's downstream!" he exclaimed. "Maybe one of those nester places!"

Almost without thinking, he had pulled his horse out of the trail and fed him the spurs, knowing only that someone was in trouble. The black ground, making deceptive shadows under the moon, flowed back under him. He heard other hoofs clatter across a stretch of hardpan

44

behind him and knew that Sally was pressing hard at his heels; and though he wanted to rein in and warn her to stay back, he knew he could not stop her. Anyway, he told himself, Sally Fox had better sense than to run right into gunfire.

He had heard no other firing, however, for a matter of minutes, though now he was getting into the breaks along the river. Whatever was going on in the night must have come to a sudden conclusion . . .

Then he saw the glow of flames against the sky ahead, and pulled in as the ground dropped away below him. Down there a house was burning, not far from the bank of the creek. Night wind whipped the flames high, sent sparks streaming upward to the new stars.

Sally pulled up beside him, and he heard her gasp of horror. "It's the Brophy place!"

"Yes," he said. And they sent their horses on again, down the slope toward the fire.

Already the house was being gutted by the flames. The windows were square boxes framing masses of seething fire. Building and furnishings were beyond any hope of salvage. Then, as Clem and the girl galloped in with a cold wind at their backs and the heat of the flames against them, a rifle spoke in the tangled shadows of the yard.

Clem had gun and belt strapped around his waist and he dug the weapon out quickly, lining down on the streak of muzzle fire. The bullet had gone very wide, and now he could make out in the tricky light a figure kneeling behind a pile of chopped wood, hunched forward over the rifle stock to make another try. But though he could have taken a good shot, he held off the trigger even before he heard Sally's piercing cry: "Don't, Clem! Don't shoot her!"

On the heels of her shout the rifle lashed again, closer now, and at the scream of the bullet Clem dragged reins and half jerked his horse around. But Sally didn't hesitate. She went flashing past Clem, straight down into the firelight and the smoking muzzle, and now she was leaping from her running mount. The figure behind the wood stack jumped up, whirling to meet her; the rifle swung like a club in an arching blow that stopped Clem Hardin's breath, so narrowly did it miss slamming against the side of Sally's head.

After that Clem was out of saddle, belatedly, and moving forward to where the two figures had joined in a struggle for the rifle. His hand found the heated barrel, seized and jerked it easily away, and tossed it to one side. Then he got the hands that had wielded the gun. They were small, and his own big fingers locked them by the wrists and he held them firmly as he gritted: "Cut this out! Cut it out, do you hear me?"

His prisoner wrenched and twisted, kicking at him. Sally exclaimed, "Please, Miz Brophy! We don't aim to hurt you!" And it must have been the girl's voice that brought a sudden end to the struggling. Clem released his grip, and at the same moment Sally Fox stepped forward and put an arm around the shoulders of the other woman.

At her touch Kate Brophy broke down completely, bowed forward, hands against her face as she sobbed hysterically.

"I thought it was them," she cried. "I thought they was coming back——"

"Here!" said Sally. The chopping block was handiest, and she led the woman to it, let her slump down there. "Don't try to talk. Just get ahold of yourself first."

Clem took a turn around the dooryard, looking at the burning house, checking hastily to see if there was anything he could save. There wasn't; he went back to Sally

and the woman, and saw that Kate Brophy had calmed
now and was talking in dead, broken sentences.

"It was Ladder! I saw the brand on one of the horses.
They came swarming in and they knocked out the windows and threw burning rags inside. They——"

She stopped. Her eyes had lit on Clem's face, and for
the first time she recognized him. "You! You're the Hardin kid! You sent them!"

"No, Miz Brophy!" Clem protested quickly. "Sally
knows I didn't. That was Meeker and Mart Raines and
their crowd—they quit me today and they've gone
bronco."

The woman was on her feet now, swaying a little as she
stood staring at him, her breast moving heavily with emotion. She was smaller than Sally, full-figured, with blond
hair that was disarrayed and shone around her head like
a wild nimbus in the light from the fire behind her. She
said, "You're lying! You hate me, and my husband—for
what happened today in town. So you sent your men to
burn us out, when no one was here to stop them but a
woman. You're like the rest of the Hardins, mean and
vicious!"

"No, no!" cried Sally. "You don't know what you're
saying!"

"I'll get her a bronc," Clem said bleakly. "There's
nothin' for her here now, and I don't think she should
be left by herself. Be better if she's handy to you and your
maw, and maybe the doc can give her something to quiet
her."

Sally said, "Yes, Clem. That's the best we can do."

With these two women for him to look after, Mart
Raines and the stolen bronc would have to wait. Clem
found the Brophys' horse, running wildly in the tiny corral behind the shed. He got blanket, saddle, and bridle

on it, and when he led the mount around for Kate Brophy to ride she stepped up into the saddle without a word.
She was dressed like Sally in jeans and shirt, and she sat
leather like a man. Clem handed up the reins. She took
them without comment, staring straight ahead; her torrent of speech had died, and now she accepted wordlessly
every suggestion of Sally and Clem, her face a mask that
showed no expression at all.

They splashed across Kettle Creek. The burning house
was only a shell now; the roof dropped in a shower of
sparks and the walls tumbled one by one into the embers.
The woman did not once look back, and soon a rise in
the ground hid that scene behind them and there was
only the moon-bright darkness around them, the stars,
and the smell of sage across the wind.

Hardly a word was spoken before the three riders
sighted the pattern of lights ahead that was Tilden town.

They rode directly to the marshal's house, but Bob Fox
was not there. "He insisted his place was at the jail,"
Sally's mother told them. "With a prisoner there and all.
So some of the boys carried him down just before supper.
I think it's awful!"

"I'll go down and see him," Sally offered. And to her
mother's question: "I'm not hungry, Maw—Shorty Jones
gave me chow at Ladder. But how about you, Miz Brophy? Won't you step in and let Maw fix you some coffee
or something? It'll brace you up."

"No," answered the blond woman, not stirring in saddle. "I want to see my husband."

"Let her come along," said Clem. "I aim for to have a
word with Bob myself."

They went the half block to the jail. A light was in the
office window; as Clem stepped down there, glass from the
shattered pane crunched underfoot. He gave Sally a hand,

and by then Kate Brophy was already dismounted. At his knock, the tired voice of the marshal said, "Come in!"

Bob Fox lay, with his shoulders propped up, on a narrow cot that was hardly long enough for his string-bean frame. A newspaper he was reading lay across his stomach, and a six-gun and box of extra shells were handy on a corner of the battered desk beside him. He said, "Evening, Clem." His shrewd eyes did not miss the battered features of the boy, but he offered no comment.

Clem murmured something, and Sally went to her father and leaned to receive his kiss. One gaunt arm around her waist, Bob looked past her at Kate Brophy. "You want to see Nat, I reckon. Get the keys off the desk there, Clem, and let her in the cell."

Brophy was clutching the strap-iron bars of the cell door, his face looking pinched and sickly in the light from the lamp on the desk. Clem found the key, turned it in the lock, and let the yellow-haired woman pass through to her husband. She had not said any word. Clem saw Brophy clutch one of her hands in both of his, his face working with the desperate expression of a man clinging to a life raft.

Turning away, he couldn't help thinking—as he had many times before—that the homesteader and the blond woman made a very strange sort of couple. Brophy had brought her back with him once from a trip to Boise, and she looked to Clem as though he must have found her in some dance hall there. Hard to imagine why she would have married such a colorless man, or let him bring her to the drab, hard life of a Kettle Creek homestead.

But none of this was any of his affair. Clem Hardin simply figured that he was young and probably had a lot to learn about the workings of people's minds and hearts.

He put the key ring back on the desk. Bob Fox said quietly, "She didn't have a gun to slip him, did she?"

"Gosh, I don't think so!" exclaimed the youngster. "I didn't search her——" And then he flushed to the roots of his tawny head, wondering what Sally would think of that remark. She didn't look as though she had heard, however, and her father only chuckled.

"Pull up chairs, kids," the marshal said then, sobering. "We better talk about some things."

Clem got one from the corner for Sally, but he didn't feel like sitting. He said, "How do you feel, Bob?"

"All right, I guess; a little shaky—that's the blood I lost. Maw says she's gonna feed me calf liver till I build up some more. Anything I hate, it's liver!" He made a face.

Sally said, frowning, "Do you have to stay here at the jail, Pop? Couldn't you get somebody else?"

"Who?" he countered. "Who that I can trust? I had to send Tom Peterson home because I knew damn well he and his friends would spring Brophy out of here in a minute if they dared. General feeling in this town is that Nat's some kind of a public benefactor——" The marshal gulped, shot a quick look at Clem. "Sorry, son! I didn't aim to say that!"

"S'all right," the youngster grunted. "I guess I know what's thought about the Hardins."

Bob Fox exclaimed quickly, "That don't include you!"

"The hell it don't." Clem's voice was heavy, lifeless. "They murdered my brothers, and I got no reason to think I wouldn't be laying alongside them now, on a table in Doc Warn's back room, had I gone into the saloon with Jap and Noah this morning."

Stirred by restless anger, he heeled away from the desk and went to stand peering out through the shattered window, out into the tangled darkness. Behind him he heard Fox's slow voice:

"The thing is, you got a chance to show now what a

Stormy Range   **51**

change of management is going to mean at Ladder. First thing this range is gonna want to know is what comes of Val Meeker and that crowd?"

Clem gave a short, hard laugh that lifted his shoulders briefly. "That's a good question," he grunted. "I tried to answer it and couldn't."

"He had a fight with Meeker," Sally explained quickly. The towheaded youth turned quickly, so that the lamplight was on his swollen, battered features. "I guess you can tell who lost," he finished for her. "They even took a Ladder horse and I wasn't able to stop them. Mart Raines forked that bronc when they raided the jail, and again tonight when they burnt out the Brophy place. No tellin' what deviltry they'll be up to next! And if I can't put a stop to that, how can I hope to prove that Ladder stands for anything decent on Kettle Creek Range?"

Bob Fox hadn't heard about the doings at Brophy's. Sally told him all she could, from what they had seen there and from what Kate Brophy had had to say. He shook his head grimly. "It's a filthy mess, and a long ways from finished. A job for the sheriff, I'd say."

Clem shrugged. "I just got a tintype of that fat buzzard, Joe Lawrence, coming out from the county seat to throw himself against an outfit like Meeker's!"

"Well, then, you see!" The marshal spread his lean hands. "If Meeker's too big for the law to tackle, how can you figure he's any responsibility of a—a——"

"A fuzz-faced kid?" Clem finished for him savagely. "Go ahead—say it! Say I ain't man enough to take the reins of a spread the size of Ladder, or do a job like the one I got ahead of me!"

His bitterness brought tears to Sally's brown eyes. Her father made an impatient gesture. "You're just all wrought up, Clem. You've had a tough day. Get some

sleep, and you'll see things different. Go on, now, and let
Maw bed you down at our place. Don't bother riding
back to the ranch tonight——"

Just then Kate Brophy called from the door of the cell,
and Clem stepped to let her out, locking the heavy door
again as she came into the office. In the harsh light of the
lamp her face looked wan as she confronted Bob Fox.
"What are you going to do about my husband?"

The marshal returned her look for a long moment.
Then he answered, "I'm going to turn him over to the
sheriff, of course, for trial. What did you expect me to
do?"

Angry fire flared in the woman's eyes, which were
slightly greenish in color. She might have been called
good-looking, in a sensuous way, but right now her face
was contorted and made almost ugly by emotion. She
said, "I expect you to see that he has adequate protection, that's what! You tricked him into going into a cell
—you said Val Meeker would let our place alone if Nat
was in jail. And so Meeker came and burned us out, since
no one was there to stop him! Meanwhile he's made one
try at the jail already; what if he comes again, and you
laid up like that? My husband wouldn't have a chance!"

"Maybe Meeker won't be back," Bob Fox suggested.
"Looks to me he's not apt to waste much more time on
Brophy—it ain't getting him any money, and I don't
reckon killing off the Hardins cuts that much ice with
him. By now he's probably more concerned with figuring
out where his next haul is coming from."

Kate Brophy made a gesture of disgust. "Talk's cheap!"
she retorted. "But I'm telling you this much: If anything
more happens to my husband while he's in your custody,
you may not have a job much longer!"

"If anything happens to him," Bob Fox corrected
tiredly, "I'll most likely be dead!"

"Well, I want to know how you aim to make sure it doesn't?"

It was Clem Hardin, surprisingly, who answered. He said, "I'll take care of Brophy."

All three turned to stare at him, the marshal shoving forward a little from his piled-up pillows. "What are you saying?" Fox demanded.

"Sally, you take our horses to the stable," Clem told the girl. "Have Limp hitch up a wagon and team and throw some old gunny sacks and stuff in the back, and tool it around here to the jail. Better run it up the alley, so as to attract as little attention as possible. We'll load Brophy into the wagon, cover him up, and I'll haul him into the county seat myself!"

The marshal shook his head a little. "But I don't get it, Clem. Why should you bother? You, of all people?"

Clem answered, "Don't you see? That's just the point. Meeker or nobody else would expect *me* to try and save Brophy's neck from a lynching."

"Yeah!" exclaimed the lawman softly. "Yeah, that's right!"

Then Sally rose and was facing Clem, her head tilted back, a shining in her eyes. "It's for Pop, isn't it?" she cried. "You'd do this for his sake!"

He backed a little, his big boots scraping the floor uncomfortably. "Well," he muttered, too embarrassed to look directly into her eyes, "it's a certainty that Brophy's friends would put the pressure on if something went wrong. Just seemed to me like I'd thought of a way to prevent it."

On the cot, Bob Fox nodded. "You have, Clem—and thanks. I'm gonna take the offer. Sally, you get down to the stable. We'll have to work by night if this is going to come off." He hesitated. "You got a long haul ahead of you, Clem. Sure you're in shape to make it?"

"Sure," said Clem Hardin, although tiredness dragged at him and his chest seemed to be getting sorer where Meeker had booted him. It hurt to breathe, a little. "I'll make it, all right. I don't really expect anything's going to happen."

Sally wasn't so sure. "You'll be careful?" she insisted, and it was only after she had Clem's promise that she left, slipping lightly through the big door. A moment later they heard her ride away, the two led horses following in the night.

Looking at Kate Brophy, the marshal said, "You'll stay with Maw tonight, of course?"

"No." She shook her blond head. "I got some money, and there's friends will get me more if I need it. I'll take a room at the hotel. Naturally I aim to be in Maxwell for the trial." She looked at Clem. "Maybe I had you wrong, kid. Maybe you ain't the same stripe as your brothers were. . . . Can I talk to Nat again for a few minutes, Marshal?"

"Sure," said Fox. "Might as well let him out of there anyway, Clem."

Clem swung the door wide and Brophy came stumbling out of the dark cubicle, blinking a little in the lamplight. Fox, a look of distaste on his gaunt features, said, "I reckon you been listening to what we plan to do. Any comment?"

The prisoner looked from one to the other and then shrugged sullenly. Fox gave a grunt: "Damn grateful cuss, ain't you?" And to Kate Brophy: "Go ahead—do what talking you got to."

It was twenty minutes later they heard the wagon rolling slowly up the alley behind the jail.

6

Bob Fox spoke gently: "All right, Clem. There they are."

Young Hardin had let himself into a chair in the corner of the room and staring at the floor, slumped there tiredly, his eyes vacant. The marshal's quiet words broke through the blanket of fatigue and emotional shock, and he lifted his head finally, with a jerk, and saw old Bob's quizzical look on him. He muttered, "Oh—oh, sure," and lurched to his feet.

"Clem," Bob Fox began, "I still don't like the idea of you——"

But the lad had already taken his hat off the corner of the desk and was turning to the door. "Be ready to travel," he told Brophy. "I'll take a look."

He stepped out, closing the door, and the cool night breeze felt refreshing as it touched him. He felt fagged out, dull-witted, his hands and feet weighted. Probably the marshal was right and he ought to be looking for a bed right now rather than planning the lone trip to Maxwell in a jolting buckboard. But he had given his word, and doggedly he was going to go ahead with it. There was a quality of stubbornness in Clem Hardin; and besides, he had failed once today, and pride insisted that he do this one job.

Light footsteps came toward him through the darkness, and there was another, uneven stride. In light from the window Clem saw Sally's sweet, serious face, Limp Kohler bobbing along behind her. "Limp's going with you, Clem," she told him quickly.

"But that ain't necessary." Clem looked at the old hostler, who returned his glance with an impassive stare.

"Any objections?" demanded Limp bluntly. "I got nothing to do this evening. Figured as you might like some company."

Clem hesitated, then shrugged without answering. So, he thought, even Limp Kohler was against him—secretly convinced the Hardin boy wasn't capable of managing this alone. . . . Clem felt a hurt, but he wouldn't argue. He heeled around and went back into the office, and Bob Fox wondered at the dark and angry look on the youngster's weary face.

"Let's go," Clem ordered. "You got a pair of handcuffs lying around, Bob?"

The marshal pointed. "In that drawer. There's a key too."

"Wait just a minute, now!" Kate Brophy flared, striding forward. "You don't aim to chain my husband up like a—a——"

"Like a common murderer?" Bob Fox finished for her dryly. "But that's what he is, ain't he? You best step aside, Miz Brophy, and kind of keep quiet. We're goin' to a lot of trouble on account of Nat."

Clem had the cuffs now. He kneed the drawer shut and with a jerk of his head toward Nat Brophy walked to the door, took a look outside before he opened it wide. Brophy hesitated, shot a quick glance at the marshal. Then he mumbled something to his wife and, turning, shuffled out past Clem to where Limp and Sally were waiting. Kate Brophy took a step to follow, but Fox stopped her. "Stay inside till they're gone. Wouldn't want anyone seeing you here—it might tip our hand."

The wheels of the buckboard grated on cinders as one of the horses stirred and stamped a little in the darkness. Enough light came through the jail window to show Clem what he was doing. He walked ahead of the others, turned at the side of the buckboard. "Climb in," he told Brophy. "Get down in the back with the blankets and stuff."

Brophy obeyed, with a grunt. As he clambered over the side of the rig Clem caught the man's wrist, snapped one of the steel cuffs around it; the other struck on iron as he fastened it to the metal framework of the seat.

"Just to be sure you won't try to sneak out over the tail gate," he said. Nat Brophy muttered something. Ignoring him, Clem grabbed the handrail and hoisted himself up onto the seat.

Sally came up close to the front wheel. "Be real careful, won't you, Clem?"

"Oh, sure. Sure." He didn't look at her as he got the reins and shook them out. The buckboard creaked and Limp swung up beside him.

"I reckon we're ready," said Limp.

Clem spoke to the horses. Sally stepped back and watched, with a frown of unhappiness, as the rig started rolling and quickly faded into the shadows.

"He acts like we were all against him," she thought. "I wish there was something I could have done or said——"

She stood like that, listening, until even the sound of the buckboard was lost in distance and the night.

Limp said: "I'll take the ribbons, Clem."

"No!" Clem snapped out the word far more vehemently than was necessary, and his hands tightened on the leathers as though he thought the old hostler might try to take them away by force. Surprised, Limp shot him a quick look. The white moon showed the tense set of Clem's jaw under the black shadow his hatbrim laid across the upper part of his face.

They had left the town behind and were pointed south-westward, following the twin ribbons of the wagon road that streaked blackly across rolling, moon-white ranges to skirt a spur of the hills coming down at their right hand. No one, seemingly, had remarked the departure of the buckboard and its passengers, and Nat Brophy still lay low in the body of the rig, burrowing into the blankets Limp had thrown there. The night had a chill in it, after the heat of the day.

Limp tried again. "I think you better let me have them leathers, Clem. Case we run into trouble, that would leave you with your hands free." He lifted the tail of his coat, showed an old six-gun shoved into his waistband. "Brought this along, but I don't reckon I'd be much help to you in that department."

This approach got results. Placated, Clem passed over the reins; and Limp accepted them with some relief, since he half expected the boy would drop asleep at any minute.

"Anybody stops us," he went on, "we'll naturally try to talk our way out of it first. We could say we're on our way to Maxwell to get—that is—well, to fetch back a couple of pine boxes from the undertaker's."

"All right, Limp."

The youngster's lifeless tone bothered Limp Kohler. He switched the reins to his free hand, rasped the palm of the other across dry, leathery cheeks. He slapped his team on the rump and looked sidelong at Clem Hardin. "You feel as low as you sound, kid?"

But Clem Hardin wouldn't be drawn out. He stared straight ahead at the road, and at the blocky shoulder of the hills under the moon. He wasn't going to open up with this old man and be talked to like a youngster. It would be too much after all that had happened, and after those few terse words in which he had read the secret opinion Sally and her father held of him—of a boy who couldn't be trusted with a man's work, or face the heavy odds confronting him now.

Thinking these bitter things, he let the rough jolting of the rig work on his tired and aching body. His head seemed to grow heavier on his shoulders. It sagged forward, jounced with the rhythm of the buckboard. He slid down in the hard seat until his bony knees were rammed against the dashboard.

There was silence, except for the noise of wheels and hoofs, until Nat Brophy shifted uneasily on his hard bed in the wagon box, eased the strained position of the hand that was coupled to the ironwork of the seat. "Hey, kid," he muttered. There was no answer, and he said louder, in his whining voice, "Kid, I—I'm damn sorry about this morning. I can't tell you how it happened—must have been out of my head, I reckon. I get blind, crazy spells like that, sometimes, when I do and say all kinds of wild and terrible things—it's as bad as having the fits. . . . Well, I guess I'm gonna pay the price for it this time—on the end of a hemp rope, most likely. But I want you to know I admire you, kid, for the way you——"

"Shut up, Brophy!" Limp Kohler snapped out of the side of his mouth. "Don't you see he ain't hearing your pretty speech? He's sound asleep—but if you don't look out you might wake him up.

"And how do you know, maybe he's just too blame tuckered out to realize there's a gun in his belt, and that the guy who murdered his brothers is handcuffed to this rig and not a soul within miles except the three of us. Was I you, I wouldn't want to remind him of that——"

A choked sound, full of startled fear, came from the prisoner in the blankets. He kept silent after that. And the buckboard rolled on under the moon with its three silent passengers. . . .

The stopping of the horses did not waken Clem Hardin, nor did the sag and creak of the springs as Limp Kohler swung down on his side of the rig. He did rouse to the sound of Limp's voice, however, lifting his head groggily and for a moment not knowing or caring where he was.

The hostler had come around the buckboard and was standing with a hand on Clem's knee, nudging him gently awake. "Hey, kid," he said. And as the boy finally shook out of sleep and focused attention on what was being said to him: "I've been looking around some and watching our back trail. There's nobody following us. It's near midnight and we've covered considerable distance."

Clem Hardin groaned and shifted out of his cramped position, scrubbed the knuckles of one hand across his aching eyes. It was very cold; the moon had set behind the blocky masses of the hills, and tumbled, broken country was dark around them.

"Where are we?" he muttered. And, coming suddenly more fully awake: "Limp! What have you stopped for? Anything wrong?"

"No, no!" said Limp Kohler. "I was just now telling you—I don't think there's gonna be any trouble. Had Val Meeker caught on to our leaving town, he'd been after us before this. But there ain't a sign."

"Oh."

Clem still sounded stupid from exhausted sleep, but Limp Kohler went on talking patiently to the boy whose face he could see as a dim blotch in the dark above him. He was afraid that if he stopped Clem would go back to sleep again.

"I think we ought to make camp. This cold is gettin' kind of rough on my arthritis, and besides, I ain't young enough to keep going all day and all night too. There's a place up yonder off the trail where we'll have water and protection in the rocks should anything happen—and it won't. So what do you say, Clem?—you're the boss."

"All right," answered the boy after another silence. He roused himself with an obvious effort. "Yeah, we'll make a stop. I—feel kind of groggy, somehow, and there's plenty blankets in the back."

Yet when they had turned the horses out of the trail, had taken the few jolting yards up to the level, boulder-sheltered spot Limp Kohler had chosen, and had un-hitched the team and made beds with the blankets from the buckboard, Clem Hardin found that the sleep had been jarred out of him and for a long time after would not return. He lay there listening to the small night sounds, to the trickle of a spring and the steady sigh of the night wind whose force was broken by the protecting circle of rocks. He watched the stars high overhead, and his mind was busy with futile thoughts.

Once a sound from the buckboard made him sit up quickly, reaching for his gun. But Nat Brophy, still cuffed to the ironwork of the seat, had apparently only turned over in his restless sleep. After a moment Clem eased back into his blankets. Near him Limp Kohler snored deeply. And presently the drug of sleep came again to Clem Hardin's battered body.

With gray dawn he woke much refreshed, to find old Limp already out of his blankets and rummaging around for something under the buckboard seat. Clem sat up, exploring his hurts with cautious fingers. His bruised face was stiff and sore enough, but the cut lip was healing and there was not much pain left in his side where Val Meeker's heavy boot had taken him.

"Morning, kid!" Limp greeted him, hopping down from the buckboard. He showed his teeth in a yellow grin as he held up half a loaf of bread and a can of airtights.

"Here's breakfast. Poor excuse for grub," he admitted, "but all I could find in a hurry, last night, to throw in."

"It's more than I counted on," said Clem, his lip stretching as he smiled. "It never'd occur to me to have brought food."

Limp was in high spirits this morning, and Clem felt considerably better himself, after his rest. They tore the bread in three pieces, opened the beans with a clasp knife, and handed the can around with the knife to use as a fork. The old man wiped his bread in the lick and gulped it down with relish. "Come noon," he promised genially, "we'll have us a real meal in Maxwell. I know an eat-shack right in back of the courthouse——"

The prisoner, reminded by this of the fate awaiting him at the county seat, told him to shut up. Limp Kohler only grinned wickedly.

A red sun was swelling out of the eastern hills as they finished their scanty breakfast. Clem gathered up the blankets, dumped them into the buckboard. At Brophy's whining request he unlocked the handcuffs and let the prisoner out of the rig to stretch his cramped legs, then he made him climb into the rig again and snapped the handcuffs on him, while Limp got the horses and put them into harness. Within an hour of waking they were on the road again.

It was to be another fine, warm day. Clem and the old man talked some as they rolled over the uneven trail; Nat Brophy slouched with his shoulders against the seat, staring moodily down the back trail, saying nothing. They were in the lower hills now, wild country of black lava, straggling juniper and jack pine, and the rock-ribbed hills rising close above them. The road lifted, and a rushing creek ran through the throat of a hollow fifty feet below them.

At a bending in the narrow trail Clem Hardin turned

for a glance at the prisoner, and something he saw then, beyond Brophy's bobbing head and the cloud of dust that boiled behind their rig, brought him half out of the seat with one hand gripping its back, hard, and a yell upon his lips.

"Hey! Riders—a bunch of them, Limp!"

"The hell!" The old man twisted about, himself, but a shoulder of rock and scrub growth cut off view as the road took another turn. Then with a grunt Kohler was on his feet, swinging leather ends at the rumps of his team. "Step out, damn you!" he shouted. "Git!"

And as the buckboard leaped sharply ahead he grunted over his shoulder: "Surely you must of seen 'em back there, Brophy! Why the hell didn't you sing out?" But the prisoner made no answer.

Gun in hand now, Clem Hardin clung grimly to the back of the seat and searched out the billowing dust behind them. Jouncing crazily, the light rig swept from side to side, taking the turns in the corkscrew trail that alternately gave him glimpses of the pursuers and then cut off his view of them. No mistake, those horses were gaining on the slower-moving buckboard; their riders were pushing them hard, and as he watched they changed from mere shadowy shapes until he could distinguish the markings on those at the fore.

He exclaimed suddenly: "No wonder he never said nothing! That ain't Val Meeker's outfit—it's a bunch of Brophy's friends!"

"So that's why they ain't shootin'. They mean to set him loose, and naturally they wouldn't take any chance of plugging him!"

"Whip up those horses!"

The old man was already whaling at them with his leathers, yelling at the top of his lungs, standing with boots wide braced. The livery horses found new speed somewhere; spinning wheels caromed off the ruts and boulders, hurling the backboard with a wild careening that threatened to smash it against the cliff at one side or send it end for end down the drop into the boiling creek below.

Nat Brophy, battered and tossed in the bed of the rattling buckboard, yelled at them above the racket: "You trying to kill all three of us? Don't be a damn fool, Kohler! You can't outrun 'em, and you know it!"

The old cripple snarled at him, "I don't like you much, Nat Brophy! I ain't happy to see them friends of yours turn you stark starin' loose——"

The trail took a sharp curve and dipped steeply, down toward the boiling creek. The running horses took it without slackening, and the buckboard struck the water like the slap of a hand. Water geysered in a silver sheet. This was a deep, barely passable ford; beyond it a mountain meadow stretched its flats, with the wagon road pointing straight away before them.

The buckboard tilted steeply as it lurched up the other bank of the creek. Clem, looking back, saw the pursuers come pouring down the pitch of the trail a half-dozen lengths behind. He spotted the lead rider—the nester, Tom Peterson. And grimly he squeezed trigger, put a bullet into the blue sky above Peterson's head.

Peterson swerved his mount but came on, the others fanning out behind him as they came onto the flats. There were six of them altogether, Clem saw in that glimpse he had. Then he was grabbing wildly for the seat as a sickening lurch of the buckboard threw him forward across the dashboard.

He heard the splintering crash as the front wheel swiped a sunken boulder and broke apart. There was the squeal of the axle end grinding stony soil, the momentum of the running team carrying them forward; but after that, braked by the crippled buckboard, the livery broncs were hauled to a stop, rearing and pawing air with their front hoofs. Seconds later the grangers were pounding in, surrounding the halted rig, broncs dripping water from their splash across the creek.

Clem Hardin clawed to pull himself erect on the sharply tilted seat. He was choked by swirling dust and the blow of the dashboard across his already sore ribs. Beside him Limp Kohler was pulling on the leathers to quiet his panicked team.

"Throw down your gun, Hardin!" Tom Peterson said.

His voice was muffled by the neckcloth he had pulled up over the bridge of his strong, beaked nose. All of them were masked that way, but Clem had no trouble recognizing most of them. There were guns in the hands of Peterson and of Luke Sands, who had reined in at the head of the buckboard team. All of the six were watching the men on the buckboard's seat intently. One led a spare horse, saddled and bridled.

Clem Hardin said, "I lost my gun." He lifted his empty hands shoulder high.

"Oh." Peterson nodded to Nat Brophy then. "Climb out of there, Nat. We've got a bronc for you."

Nat Brophy lifted his manacled wrist. "I'm chained down," he said.

"Give him the key," Peterson told Clem; then he changed that. "Wait! I'll find it myself." He reined in closer to the wrecked vehicle and, leaning from saddle, reached to shove his free hand into Clem's pockets, one after the other.

The boy submitted to this indignity. Suddenly he was trembling, with baffled rage; it ran through his thin body, caused his lifted hands to shake and his bruised lips to twitch spasmodically. And Tom Peterson, seeing that, thought it was fear that did it.

"Hell, kid," he muttered. "We ain't gonna hurt you!" The mask hid the sneer on his lips but it could not hide the mocking look in the eyes so close to Clement's. Then he had the key, and he straightened, tossed it to Brophy, who caught it. "Hurry up, Nat."

Clem heard the click of the locks, heard Brophy's grunt as the man freed himself. He knew he should speak, to remind these men of the enormity of what they were doing and the punishment the law would have for them. But his mouth and throat were dry as cotton and his tongue could find no words. He could only sit there trembling with fury, and with that old feeling of childish impotence paralyzing him.

On the seat beside him Limp Kohler had dropped the reins and had his arms lifted, hands like arthritic claws at either side of his scowling, forward-thrust head. Now he shifted around quickly and gritted at Brophy: "You best stay where you are if you want to live, mister!"

The prisoner was on his feet, ready to vault down from the tilted floor of the rig. Something in Limp's voice made him hesitate, glance nervously at Tom Peterson.

"Hell! He can't stop you!" Peterson gestured with his gun. "Come on, Nat! Don't take all day!"

"*I said no!*" And with the words old Limp Kohler's crippled right hand was moving down, whipping aside the tail of his coat and clawing at the butt of the gun he had behind his waistband. Somebody let a squawk as they saw that weapon. Limp had it dragged out now, thumb earing back the hammer as he swung the muzzle around toward Nat Brophy. "You murderin' hellion! Stay where you——"

Just what happened then was a thing no man could describe accurately when it was over. It seemed to Clem that Luke Sands probably fired the first shot, and that his bullet, striking Limp Kohler, jarred the old man's thumb off the hammer of his cocked gun. The two shots came so close together they blended their shocked sound. The blast of Limp's weapon almost deafened Clem; then, in dazed horror, he saw the old man slowly crumple, topple over against him there on the tilted seat.

Moving woodenly, he caught the slight body of the man, nose and eyes stinging from the fog of burnt gunpowder. And then, slowly, he lifted his head to stare at the mounted men. "He's dead!" Clem said thickly, in a dazed voice. "You've killed him!"

Saddle horses and buckboard team were stamping and rearing, terrified by the nearness of the shots. The buckboard slewed around, jarred to a stop. It was then, as Peterson and another shouted jumbled words and swung down from their saddles hurriedly, that Clem Hardin had his first intimation that other damage had been done.

They were lifting Nat Brophy's unconscious body out of the dust. Blood made its smear across the side of his head, showing where the bullet from Limp's gun had struck him. Tom Peterson's voice was grim as he said hurriedly: "Still alive, but he's bad hit!" He looked around quickly, then jerked his head at Luke Sands. "Come here, Luke! You got a good horse—take him up on the saddle with you."

Sands fumbled to shove his smoking gun away and reined wide of the nervous buckboard team to come around to Peterson's side. Leaning a little from saddle, he stammered, "I didn't aim to do it, Tom! I never meant to start shootin'——"

"The damage is done!" Tom Peterson grunted impatiently. "Now hurry up! Take him!"

As they helped lift the hurt man up onto Sands's saddle, another of the men had reined in close to the buckboard and taken a careful look at the body of the hostler. "Limp's dead, all right!" he exclaimed in a frightened voice. "There'll be hell to pay now!"

Not answering, Peterson turned and stepped up to his own saddle. He started to swing away from the buckboard, paused and gave Clem Hardin a long look as though he would say something but didn't know what. Clement, too stunned for speech, returned his look. Then, with a sharp jerk at the reins, the leader swung away. "Let's go!" he muttered. "We can't do anything here!"

Moments later Clem was alone with the body of Limp Kohler in his arms as the knot of masked riders went drumming back along the trail as they had come. They splashed across the creek, went up the steep rise into the timber of the hill. It was a long time before the lad on the seat of the broken rig could shake himself loose of his horror of the thing that had been done here.

7

A FIERCE sun sent its heat smashing down on silent hills, penetrating the high, pungent haze of distant smoke, as Clem Hardin's horse lifted him finally up the stony throat of a gully and out onto a lip of rimrock. He stopped the animal, let a spent glance run across the pine-stippled reaches that broke in waves of light and shadow at his feet. Far, far below the hills played out, meeting the pinkish dun of the flatlands.

There wasn't any sound except, on the slope behind him, the dry creaking of a dead tree stirred by the wind. This was so much like a barn door sagging on unoiled hinges that Clem found himself looking over his shoulder, hunting out the source of it; he spotted it quickly—a whitened snag, still standing with dead roots anchored in the rocky soil.

He ran a sleeve across his face to mop away dirt and sweat and came down wearily from the bare back of his horse. It was one of the buckboard team, and he had taken it out of harness and with improvised reins and no kind of saddle had spent three grueling, toilsome hours. The results were nothing.

The riders he sought to trail had soon split apart and taken to the timbered ridges, guessing perhaps that Clement would try to follow and determined to throw him off. But a dogged determination had kept him hunting for the sign of Luke Sands's mount, carrying the added burden of Nat Brophy. He had found it, and followed it

69

miles higher and deeper into the hills; but now the track had played out and he knew he must turn back.

It was a hard thought—almost the crowning defeat of all he had endured in these two terrible days. One more failure chalked against him—and, worst of all, Limp Kohler dead; murdered, trying to help with the job that had been too big for Clement Hardin.

He let himself down upon a rock, dropped his head tiredly upon folded arms. It all flooded in upon him then, and with the salt of sweat upon his tongue he sat there savoring the acrid flavor of self-disgust. The first revulsion passed and he lifted his head, stared with hollow eyes upon the far-spread panorama below him. The horse stomped at his back, wandered away to pull at the thin rock grass. But the impulse of movement seemed dead in Clement Hardin; he sat motionless while the sun wheeled overhead and shadows ebbed and flowed across the spear-topped pines. *You're man-size,* the voice had spoken coldly within him, *but you haven't got the makings of a man.* . . . And he accepted this, and yet some strange, consoling wisdom promised that this hour was the worst that he would ever know, and that somehow he would live beyond it and the experience would give him strength.

For time does not halt, even when the spirit dies in man; and at length Clem had to climb back onto his feet and pick up the threads of his existence. It was the friendship of Limp Kohler which even now pulled him past this crisis; for Limp still lay under blankets in the wrecked buckboard where Clem had left him, and there was one last service remaining to pay his friend.

Lamplight spotted the windows and doors of town as he rode in through the fall dark, the lead horse with its grim burden trailing. He approached circumspectly, avoiding the main streets and the square, aiming for the shack where Doc Warn lived alone near the edge of the settlement. The doctor served the range as undertaker, and he alone could render any further service to old Limp. Clem halted under the cottonwood that fronted the clapboard building, and he looked a long time at the dimly lit window before he lifted his voice in a shout.

After a moment the doctor came out, the sagging screen door squealing protest. "I've got Limp Kohler's body," Clem Hardin said out of piled shadows. "He was killed this morning on the Maxwell road."

A gusty exclamation broke from the doctor, and a half-dozen questions followed it. Clem Hardin sighed as he swung down to help ease Limp's body off the back of the livery horse and take it inside the shack. This was just the beginning, he knew; there would be no end of questions now. He put the doctor off shortly. "It's a long yarn, Doc. I got to leave it up to Bob Fox to decide how much of it he wants told. You ask him, will you?"

Warn did not like this answer, but Clem left him with it and went next to the livery barn. More questions, here, about Limp Kohler's absence, and the buckboard which had been borrowed and not returned. "Ask the marshal," he said stonily. "I'll pay to have your rig brought back and patched up; send me the bill. Right now I'm dog-gone tired. I want my bronc." He left the proprietor in a bad mood and went to the stall, where his sorrel greeted him with a pleased whicker.

He threw on saddle and gear, moving woodenly, his mind not on what he was doing. He was a coward, he decided. He ought to go directly and make his report to Fox, and yet somehow that was a thing he just couldn't do. Because Sally would be there, and he couldn't face her now. So, being a coward, he decided he would take the coward's way. He fished paper and pencil out of his pocket and, propping the paper against his saddle, laboriously scrawled out a terse report on what had happened.

At the end he wrote, "I am some anxious to see how things are going out at the ranch, so that is why I am not stopping to make talk with you tonight." He figured the marshal, and Sally too, would know this for a lie and that they would come close to guessing his real reasons for avoiding them. But they already had him pegged for what he was. It didn't matter much what kind of proof he gave them now.

Clem folded the paper and gave a kid half a dollar to take it to the marshal's house. *That's that,* he thought afterward, and led his sorrel down the straw-littered aisle and out into the clean-smelling night air.

And on the sidewalk just before the wide door he met Kate Brophy.

They both halted, taken aback, and stared at each other in the fan of light from a nail-hung lantern over the runway. Kate looked altogether different from the way she had last night; then she had been distraught and somewhat bedraggled-looking, but she had had twenty-four hours since to get a hold of herself and she had done a thorough job of it.

Moving into town must have prompted the change in her, Clem thought. She had on a sleek-looking dress that looked new, and her yellow hair was carefully done, her face fixed up with rouge and rice powder. She had a shawl about her shoulders, held by a pin at her throat. She looked very sure of herself now—except that this unexpected meeting with Clement Hardin had caught her unprepared and she showed her startled surprise.

"Hullo!" exclaimed Clement foolishly.

For a moment she only stared, the hostility plain in the stiffening of her face and body. Her painted mouth opened, closed again as she seemed to hunt for words. At last she said harshly, "So you're back! It didn't take you long."

"To go to Maxwell?" All at once Clem Hardin felt about a million years old, and filled with a cynical wisdom. He felt that he could read every thought inside that yellow-topped head tilted toward him, and yet he found no pleasure in this. He almost smiled, mouth twisted a little at one corner. "You're just burning up with curiosity, ain't you? Peterson and the others ain't came back yet, and you're dyin' to know how your plans worked out."

Her breast lifted on a quick intake of breath. "I don't savvy what you're talking about!" she exclaimed; but he knew she did.

"There's only one way Peterson could have known what we cooked up in the jail last night," said Clem, thinking his way through to how it must have been. "You sent them after me and Limp, to take Brophy away from us. Well, they got him all right! It didn't matter to you none if somebody was to get hurt, or even killed——"

She slapped him. There was strength in her arm and she put it all behind the palm that lashed openly across his cheek. Clem's head jerked with the blow and it startled him to silence; he stood there with the sting of it ringing in his head.

Kate Brophy's shawl had slipped with the movement. She caught it about her, and there was a blaze of hatred in her eyes. Clem started to lift a hand toward his stinging face, dropped it again. "What good did that do?" he muttered finally.

"You damned cheeky kid!" she spat at him in a voice vibrant with scorn. "You think you're a sure-enough man, don't you? Well, you just keep your lip to yourself.

And you better not go around repeating what you just said where the marshal could hear you and maybe start getting ideas. You understand?"

Clem said stolidly, "I reckon maybe the marshal can figure things out for his ownself."

Her eyes narrowed as she apparently considered this. Suddenly, without another word, she tossed her head and went past him, her full skirt swishing against his legs, the cheap scent she wore clinging briefly behind her. Clem turned to watch her go, still standing there for a moment when the sound of her heels clicking had faded along the walk and he was alone in the spray of lantern light, by the livery archway.

He glanced around then, a little furtively. He hoped nobody had witnessed that scene, and the slap. No telling what construction the bums who hung around the stable would have put on it, what sniggering comments they might have made. But he saw no one, and quickly turned to his sorrel saddler, scowling as he reached for stirrup and twisted it to receive his foot.

It didn't seem to matter much, knowing he had guessed right about Kate Brophy's part in the kidnapping of her husband. The leaden mood he was in, nothing carried very much importance. He supposed that being dog-tired was a good part of this; if he could get out to Ladder and into a bed, the drugging fog of sleep would probably leave things looking a little different in the morning and he would begin to see some kind of program ahead of him.

So, with the horse restless under him after its day of inactivity, Clem Hardin took the north road out of Tilden town—and, on a wide, barren flat just beyond the straggle of buildings that marked its limits, came upon Ed Pringle's Green Parrot dive, alive with lights and noise and the jangle of a coin-operated piano. Boisterous figures of men moved behind the opened windows and across the veranda that extended across the inner angle of the L-shaped building. A line of hipshot horses stood at the tie poles, vagrant rays of the light from the windows glinting on metal saddle fixings. Something in that made him rein down the sorrel while he studied the gambling joint with tired, bloodshot eyes. It held a kind of fascination.

Suddenly a violence of trembling started in him, spreading through all his long limbs. His jaw clamped, teeth grinding to keep him from chattering until the muscles ached. A drop of cold sweat started below his left armpit, trickled slowly from rib to rib.

"Damn you!" he gritted, cursing his own weakness and the fear that had risen chokingly inside him. "You made a brag—what are you going to do about it? This is the last chance to break your run of failure and show whether you've got anything in you or not."

Next moment, although every fear-stretched nerve in him fought against it, he had pulled his sorrel to the left, was holding it that way, resolutely, walking the bronc straight toward the noisy, light-splashed building. With his free right hand he fumbled at the jutting six-gun handle in his belt holster, lifting it and loosening it in the leather. It felt cold, and heavy to his stiff fingers. He rode to within a dozen feet of the veranda railing and then he dismounted; his legs seemed uncertain of whether they would hold him up or not, his knees feeling as though they were completely unhinged and ready to fold in the wrong direction.

It was not nerve, but a kind of fatalism, that drove him on—a certainty that if he failed this challenge he would never again be able to come to satisfactory terms with himself.

Drunken laughter, the clatter of the piano washed out at him through the open windows. But no one appeared to have noticed his coming; the veranda happened just then to be empty. He dropped reins to hold his sorrel ground-anchored, pulled at his belt to hitch the heavy holster into better position. Then, moving stiffly, he started down along the line of horses at the rack, looking for the one he knew he would find there.

The crunch of his boots on hardpan seemed jarringly loud, and the scrape of his spurs, the creaking of his gun harness. Two steps and he had halted, poised there in the faint light from the veranda windows as he battled again with himself not to turn and scramble into saddle, take his flight. He thought grimly, *You're not—you're not!* Somehow he made himself go on.

A chestnut bay was halfway down the line of tied horses. He couldn't read the brand in that unsure light, so he fished a match from his pocket and thumbed it into life, stepping in close for a look at the sleek left shoulder. The animal must have smelled the fear in him, because it shied, nudging its neighbor and sending a stir of movement down the line.

But by now Clem Hardin was certain of the bronc—he would have been even without the quick glimpse he had of the Ladder burn it wore. He muttered hoarsely, "Hold it! Easy, fellow!" as he dropped the match into the dust and put a boot upon it. Then he had edged in beside the chestnut, taken the reins, and was about to jerk them loose from the gnawed pole when he thought suddenly, *It don't settle nothing if I just take him and sneak away. They got to know about it——*

The panic surged up again, like an unsettled sickness in the belly. *Come on!* he prodded himself. *Come on, now! You're doin' all right so far——*He lifted his head for a look at the empty veranda above him. And went numb with panic as he saw it was no longer empty.

One of the two men there was the solid frame of Val

Meeker, leaning forward with his hands spread upon the rail and his eyes turned squarely on the shadowy shape of the youngster among the horses at the rack. He and his companion must have heard the noise the stirring broncs made and stepped out to investigate, their coming covered by the shift of hoofs on the hard earth. Meeker said harshly, "Who's down there? What's goin' on?"

Clem had frozen, not able to move or speak or force a thought through the meshed gears of his brain. He had an insane hope that if he kept still, the big man would think he had been mistaken and go back inside, not seeing him there by the pole. But this hope was shattered when a door behind Meeker was thrown suddenly open, a bright shaft of lampglow slid out across the veranda and the dust, and Hardin stood clearly revealed, limned by the wash of light.

A surprised grunt broke from Meeker; he straightened, his hands dropping from the veranda railing. "The kid! It's the Hardin brat! Well, what do you know!" The teeth gleamed faintly beneath his roached mustache, in a snort of amusement.

Other men were coming through the open door, Ed Pringle among them—a cold-eyed man with the secrecy of manner that marked a professional gambler. The lamps inside etched them dimly as they crowded along the railing, boots scuffing the warped boards of the veranda. They were staring at Clem, everyone of them, the full force of the light holding him pinned squarely before their eyes.

Then one yelled in drunken rage, "What the hell! That's my bay he's got!"

Clem Hardin knew that this was the moment. His hand tightened on the reins of the chestnut convulsively, so that the animal tossed its head and jerked his arm sharply. Then he had a hold of himself and his voice was speak-

ing, a dead man talking there in the dust: "No! He belongs to Ladder—and I'm taking him. You aim to stop
me, Mart Raines?"

"Why, you damned, cheeky——"

Raines was drunk, maybe, but liquor didn't affect the
control of his gun arm. Suddenly he had struck for the
gun in his tied-down cutaway leather holster, and a cold
fatality settled upon Clem as he saw death rushing upon
him. What he did then was almost without conscious
volition or thought.

He dropped to his knees, right hand fumbling for gun
butt. He could never have held a gun steady, but the tie
pole was solidly set into the hard earth, and it was across
this brace, level with his eyes as he knelt there, that he
dropped the barrel of the gun as he whipped it up from
holster. The flash of Mart Raines's weapon was blinding
red fire; the bullet ripped the air above him at a point
where his head would have been had he stayed upon his
feet. And it was at the blinding smear of the flash that
Clem Hardin aimed when his own finger cramped the
stiff mechanism of the trigger.

Twice he shot, and a cloud of cordite swept against his
face and choked him. Blinking tears, he saw the incredible thing that happened then—saw Mart Raines, the gunman, jerk and sag, and buckle forward across the veranda railing. One of his neighbors might have caught him
and broken his fall, but they seemed as helpless with
astonishment as Clem Hardin himself. No hand was
raised; and Mart Raines jackknifed, tumbled limply to
the hard earth at the foot of the veranda. Lay there in a
sprawl, not a dozen feet away from Clem.

He was dead. Clem Hardin had killed a man. . . .

The youngster shook his head, as though to clear it of
shock, and slowly lifted his glance again toward the men
on the veranda. All along the tie pole the frenzied horses

were plunging and snorting, trying to tear free, but nothing stirred up there beyond the railing. Every gun remained in holster; every eye held as though frozen upon
the slim youth kneeling in the dust among the pitching
horses in the line-up.

And from somewhere a surging exultation rose within
him—a wild thing, almost stronger than the horror at
sight of the man his hand had destroyed. It carried him
on against the extreme danger that still confronted him,
gave him the audacity he needed.

"Is there anybody else?" he demanded in a clear, strong
voice, his smoking gun still menacing the half-dozen men
along the veranda rail above him. "Anybody that thinks a
Ladder mark on a horse don't mean it belongs to me?"

Not even a boot sole scraped the timbers of the porch,
not a hand moved nearer to a gun. One or two of the men
cut quick glances toward Val Meeker, but even he appeared too astounded by the thing he had seen to jar
himself into motion.

"*Anybody?*" Clem repeated sharply.

Then, despite a hundred qualms, he rose deliberately,
shoved his gun into holster, and, turning, jerked the
chestnut bay loose from the pole and walked over to his
horse, leading it. The sorrel had held place, anchored on
trailing leathers. With all the appearance of outward
calm, Clem shoved his boot into stirrup and swung as-
tride. But his muscles knotted in a kind of spasm as Val
Meeker's hard voice cut the silence:

"That's a fifty-dollar saddle you're stealin'!"

Easy, now easy! Hardin cautioned himself, and forced
a coolness into the turn of his head as he looked at the
man. But then he understood. Meeker hadn't gone for a
gun; he was not going to, but was only resorting to
tongueplay in a last-minute effort to save face before his
men and the other onlookers. And sensing this with some

unknown center of wisdom, Clem Hardin was able to reply with an undisturbed assurance:

"It's a fifty-dollar horse; makes us even. Besides—Raines won't need no saddle, the place he's gone to." He added heavily, "You can all of you end up in hell, if you want to. At least this cuts the very last string tying you to Ladder."

He kicked the sorrel and he rode away from there, the bay trailing. A stunned silence followed him, and that was all. In a matter of minutes he was in the trail again, and a rise of ground dropped the lights of Pringle's somewhere at his back.

Only then did the reaction hit him, with a kick that turned him weak so that he had to cling, doubled up, to the saddle horn while the nauseous shakiness went through him. The pommel was slick with the sweat of his hands when he straightened again and ran a sleeve across his face.

"That was cuttin' it thin," he muttered aloud into the darkness. "Was it really *me* that did that?"

Afterward, not knowing whether that crowd of toughs might be after him shortly to remedy the poor showing they had made, he went up the north trail at a hard gait, laying distance behind the hoofs of the two broncs. The moon traveled with him, its frosty brightness upon the land.

Clem Hardin had never been so physically tired, so whipped and thrashed out in body and spirit. Yet a deep satisfaction was spreading somewhere within him. He had stood up to Val Meeker; he had—yes, he had beaten a man who meant to kill him!

Driven by a most elemental need for self-respect, he had made the first breach in the garment of insufficiency that hampered him. He was not afraid now of tomorrow.

8

When he woke next morning in his own room at Ladder he wondered why he should be so utterly used up and exhausted. He had pretty well recovered from the beating administered by Val Meeker two days ago, but what he felt was something other than that. Then memory of last night flooded in upon him and Clem Hardin understood. He dressed slowly, busy with thoughts about the future and the immediate problems that confronted him.

No expectation had ever been farther from his mind than that he should one day be the only surviving Hardin, the sole master of Ladder brand. He knew, of course, the general problems of the ranch—the size of its herds, the question that had been posed by diminishing water supplies as homesteaders encroached on Kettle Creek and as late summer's drought dried up the few natural tanks and springs. But his half brothers had not encouraged him to take much active interest in the management of affairs, and he had drifted into indifference, staying on Ladder because it was his home and the only life he knew and because his friends were on this range, but supposing that in another year or two he would be drifting on somewhere and leaving the ranch to the heavy-handed Jap and Noah, and to the tough crews they hired.

Now, however, Ladder and all its pressure of problems had been dumped into his lap and, inexperienced as he was, he would have to start at once working toward some program. The first need, he supposed, would be to wrangle some kind of crew to replace Meeker's outfit. This wouldn't be easy. Riders were short that season, and drifters were not prone to sign with an owner faced with as many potential enemies as Clement Hardin. They'd hear about his troubles with the nesters, and with Meeker, and they wouldn't hire. He was scowling over this problem as he strapped on his gun belt—an essential article of clothing with him now—and went down through the empty, silent house.

In the kitchen, redolent with simmering coffee and a big boilerful of oatmeal that steamed at the back of the smoking wood range, Shorty Jones greeted him with a nod and a terse bit of information. "Couple of the boys are out there."

"Huh?"

"Tally Brown and Chuck Yancey. I dunno what brought 'em or what they want, but they're waitin' to see you. Been here an hour."

He stabbed a broad thumb toward the door, and stepping to the opening, Clem looked and saw the two men, hunkered in a patch of sun near the bunkhouse with their horses snubbed to a corral post. They were smoking as they waited, settled into a patience that seemed capable of lasting for an unnamed stretch of time—the monotonous life of a cowhand is a developer of such endurance. Clem Hardin worried a lip for a moment, trying to assign a cause for their presence; then he shrugged and told Shorty over one shoulder, "Pour me a cup of coffee and let it be cooling. I'll find out what's on their minds."

The old cook's sour warning came as he stepped out into the sunlight: "Watch 'em, boy! Those two didn't come onto this range with Val Meeker, but they certainly left with him. I don't trust none of that bunch."

Neither did Clem, but curiosity took him across the barren yard. It was a fine morning, the sky pale blue with a few streaks of cloud like white brush strokes across the blue. The sun was warm, but a breeze held the sheathed edge of a knife. The smoke tang was only faintly perceptible; the distant fire must be burning itself out. Maybe there had been a rain in the hills.

Brown and Yancey eased to their feet as Clem approached, throwing away their cigarettes. They were a nondescript pair of hands who had been on Ladder pay roll for maybe six months at the time of Jap and Noah's murder. Hardin halted a couple yards from them and said shortly, "Well?"

They exchanged a look which wordlessly nominated Talley Brown their spokesman. He tongued his lower lip and blurted, "We was at Pringle's last night——"

"I thought I seen you," said Clem coldly, unyielding. "Did you boys get Mart Raines buried?"

Another exchange of glances. They were having rough going, and it began to dawn on Clem, with a certain wonder, that these two were afraid of him. Doggedly, Tally Brown went on. "We didn't wait to find out. We left pretty quick after—after it happened. We're fed up with Meeker and that crowd of his," he ended, blurting it. "We want to go back to work!"

Clem was left staring. He couldn't comprehend for a long moment that Brown had really said this—or, for an even longer one, just what it had meant. Apparently he had done more last night, there in the dust before the gallery at Pringle's, than he dreamed. He had won back a measure of his own self-respect; but what he saw here was a tribute to the respect his actions had awakened in other men.

He was silent so long that the two men took his stare for a frown of dismissal. Tally Brown lifted a gaunt shoulder and turned away; Chuck Yancey scraped a rope-hard hand across the beard stubble of his broad jowl.

"Okay, okay!" he grunted. "I didn't hardly think you'd want to take us back."

Clem found his tongue. "You boys had breakfast?" They halted doubtfully. The lean-faced Brown shook his head. Hardin said, "Come on and have Shorty fix you up, then. We got to do some riding this morning . . ."

The faces of the pair cracked, slowly widened into grins. "Right with you, boss!" said Brown.

No one had ever called Clem Hardin "boss." He blinked a little, and some new emotion began to swell inside him. Heeling abruptly, he led his two-man crew up to the kitchen, where Shorty Jones waited in the doorway, a scowl on his ruddy face.

Clem hadn't known he was so hungry. He bolted the food Shorty set in front of him on the oilcloth-covered table, and rose feeling stuffed around the belly and without the tiredness that had hung to him when he woke that morning. He told the pair of wranglers, who were still eating, "I'll get a rig on my sorrel and we'll hit the hills. Come down to the corral when you're finished."

They nodded and he went out, meeting Shorty with an armload of split pine from the woodpile. The cook stopped him, scowling, to jerk his head toward the kitchen and say sharply, "How about that pair? You sure of 'em? Could be they're a plant, you know, sent back here on Val Meeker's orders."

"I thought of that," Clem admitted. "But—shucks, there wouldn't be any point in him doing that. And besides, these fellows never were a part of his crowd."

"Just the same," the old cook warned, "I'd keep an eye on 'em."

"I mean to," said Hardin, and went down to the corrals.

He had the sorrel under blanket and saddle and was jerking up the cinches—an exertion that put only a dull pain in his side where Val Meeker had booted him—when his men came trailing down from the kitchen, rolling smokes and wiping mouths on sleeves. At Clem's orders they unlashed their war sacks and toted them into the bunkhouse—"You'll have the place to yourselves," Hardin told them. When they returned their youthful boss called them over for a conference.

"I want to know just what went on the night before my brothers were killed," he said flatly. "They never used to let me in on their plans, but I know for a fact that Meeker and half the crew were gone from the bunkhouse that night, and I heard later they were out cuttin' wire. How about it? Were you two riding with them?"

Yancey shook his head. "No—Meeker hand-picked his men that night, and he wouldn't have called on us. But I heard their brags later. They said they'd had orders to pour it on that nester layout and bring things to a head, and that they'd done a hell of a good job."

"Well, they brought things to a head, all right!" Clem observed grimly. He added, "Hit saddle, then. We'll have a look."

He took the lead and they pulled away from the ranch, angling south and east toward the nearest of the nester places along Kettle Creek. Clem studied the range, noting how the grass was browning out, how the few creeks on which Ladder graze depended were mostly cracked stretches of mud at this tail end of summer dryness. He frowned at the thirsty beef he saw, and cast an anxious look at the peaks of the western skyline.

A few clouds up there, but nothing that promised any hope. And either they must have rain soon or something drastic would have to be done. He was mulling the problem as the trio came in toward Peterson's, the first of the homestead layouts.

From a distance they could tell that disaster had struck

the gleaming line of fence. Long stretches of it were out, the juniper posts uprooted. Wood and wire had been pulled aside into tangled heaps, so as to protect stock from tearing their legs upon the cruel barbs; and the shapes of grazing cattle dotted the acres of Peterson's green wheat.

Clem had halted, the riders flanking him. "Well, there it is," he said bleakly. "And if it's like that all along the line, no wonder the nesters went on the warpath. I dunno. I dunno how Jap and Noah thought they could get away with a thing like this—I don't figure what got into their minds——" He choked off, seeing here a token of the hatred which the name of Hardin had earned for itself. Then he shrugged away the futile thought. "Come on!" he grunted, putting his sorrel forward.

"What's the program?" Brown wanted to know.

"Every head of Ladder stock has got to be shoved back onto Ladder range, of course, where they belong."

The puncher looked dubious. "Hard to keep 'em there, with the fences down and better grass and water and standing wheat on the other side of the line. We gonna turn fence builder for a bunch of nesters, maybe?"

"I dunno yet," Clem answered shortly. "But what Ladder did it's up to me to undo——"

Chuck Yancey cut in: "Oh-oh! Lookit!"

Heading around a steep outcropping of lava rock, they had crossed a sharp rise, and now a wider stretch of country lay before them—as far as Kettle Creek itself, which they could glimpse as it snaked its way through the steep gorge of its channel. And now, too, they saw the riders putting their broncs through a gate into the pasture below them. There were half a dozen horsemen, and another man who handled a farm wagon and team jouncing along in the wake of the rest. Sunlight glinted from rolls of wire stowed in the wagon box.

Hardin said, "Looks like the nesters are going to work to fix things themselves. Well, we'll go down and lend 'em a hand—show 'em our intentions are good."

They went in at a lope. Below them the farmers had touched up their horses and were spreading out, riding straight at the grazing Ladder stock with hats swinging and yells lifted, to start them moving toward the down fence and their own side of the boundary. They rode awkwardly, grangers unaccustomed to the saddle and not much experienced at working stock; and they were apparently too absorbed in their work to see the approach of the trio of cowmen. Coming in, Clem noticed the blond head and red face of the Swede, Tom Peterson, leading the others.

The scattered cattle had turned and begun to drift loosely in front of the yelling horsemen, breaking into a shuffling, lumbering run toward the barrier. But at the last moment one big steer, reluctant to leave good grass for the burned-out range beyond the fence, balked and came wheeling around. He spotted a gap in the line of his persecutors, lunged through this and back toward the wheat field, and three other animals, with the instincts of their kind, quickly followed his lead into the break he had found.

On the instant, Tom Peterson mouthed a curse and, yanking a six-gun, emptied it at the steers that had got past him, back into the wheat. The shots ripped flatly against the morning; two of the steers went crashing down. And then Clem Hardin, face tense and white with fury, had roweled his bronc and was galloping in fast.

The frightened steers scattered out of his way. He came up on the blind side of Peterson, and the first the Swede knew of his presence was the sudden grip of Hardin's fingers, seizing his gun arm and wrenching him almost out of saddle.

Peterson gave a bellow and clutched for the horn to hold himself in leather as the smoking gun went spinning from his hand. Pulling away, he brought his horse around, got it settled as Clem snapped hotly, "Damn you! What's the idea, slaughtering my cattle?"

The farmer returned his hot glare with a red face gone even redder from anger. Peterson was a big man, hard-muscled, beefy, and large-handed. A curling mat of yellow hair showed below the V of his open shirt collar. His thick chest was swelling with his heavy breathing now and the cords stood out in his neck.

He said hotly, "I'd be in my rights if I shot every stinkin' Ladder steer that you Hardins shoved through my cut fence!"

"And I tell you I had nothing to do with it!" Clem retorted flatly. He indicated his companions. "Us three are here to help move my stock back where it belongs. But I warn you—you better not let me see you using a gun on any more of them, just because you lack the savvy to handle them!"

He kicked his bronc past the glowering Swede and rode toward the two steers Peterson had shot. One was dead, but the other lay thrashing and making piteous sounds of pain, the blood running from its smashed leg. Clem drew his gun and, leaning from saddle, dispatched the suffering beast. His face was still pale with fury as he straightened then and turned back to confront the grangers.

The rest of them had moved up to join Peterson, their leader; the man on the wire wagon was standing on the seat of his halted rig, watching. But Clem Hardin's two riders were there too, and they had hands on holstered gun butts and were obviously waiting for any trouble the nesters wanted to start.

"Well?" Clem snapped. He was too angry to remember,

in that moment, that he was only a beardless youngster facing grown men with a temerity that had not been in him days ago. He was too wrought up to wonder at this, or to question whether there might be anything ludicrous in the picture he presented. Apparently the farmers didn't think so. They returned his dark look with the sullen respect they might have shown a man of their own status, and a dangerous one at that. And now one of the older of the group—a white-maned homesteader named Billy Ruby, whose face was a leather-dark mass of wrinkles—cleared his throat.

"Go easy, Pete," he told the fuming Peterson. "No sense picking a fight with him—you heard what he did at Pringle's last night! Hardin says he wants to work with us. Looks like we ought to let him show if he means it or not."

His conciliatory words had their effect. Clem saw it in the faces of the other nesters, and then even Tom Peterson showed signs of backing down. He threw a sour look around at his companions and shrugged heavily. "Well, if that's how the rest of you feel about it," he grunted. "But, hod damn it, he better not put his hands on me again! If he tries it I'll——"

"You'll what?" Chuck Yancey prodded. A grin split his stubble face. "Too bad none of you sodbusters couldn't of been there last night, when the kid hung crape on Mart Raines and that whole Meeker tough crowd stood back and never lifted a hand against him. There wasn't none of *them* wanted to make big, hard talk, after that!"

Clem's face had taken color. He broke in sharply, "Cut it out, Chuck! Forget about last night—I don't want anybody tryin' to build me up into a gunfighter or anything because of a lucky shot!" Suddenly conscious of the smoking gun in his hand, he hastily shoved it deep into holster, reined away.

"Come on—let's start moving cattle!"

The three from Ladder fell upon the scattered steers with a whoop and with saddle ropes swinging; and the cattle, sensing that these were men who knew their business, gave way with little balking. One old fellow tried to change pace and bolt past Clem's sorrel, but the wise cow pony shifted quickly, shouldered into the steer, and almost tumbled him. The critter came out of a stumble, shaking his head, and meekly went trailing after the rest that Brown and Yancey were chousing out of the young wheat.

A grudging respect showed in the farmer group as they compared the efficiency of these cowmen with their own clumsy efforts. Then Bill Ruby, the peacemaker, said, "Well, are we gonna just sit here?" and they jogged their mounts forward to lend a hand. Tom Peterson got down, picked up his gun and blew the dust out of it and dropped it into holster; he was still scowling, and evidently he didn't like the way that scene had gone.

Working together, cowmen and farmers quickly had the stock cleared out of there, and then the wagon, with its spools of gleaming wire, was maneuvered into position and repairing of the fence begun. It was hot, sweaty work. When the damage had been remedied at Peterson's they moved on to the next place, and the process was repeated.

There were eight homestead claims strung along this side of the river, including those of the absent Luke Sands and Nat Brophy. All of them had been struck in Ladder's night raid, in what had certainly been a dangerous and open bid for war. It appalled Clement to consider the ruthless impulse behind the blow; he didn't know what wild ideas could have been in the minds of Jap and Noah, ordering it.

He had seen a turn for the worse in his half brothers, though, during these last weeks. It shouldn't have been hard to tell that a break of some sort was coming. The drought, the straining of feelings between Ladder and its neighbors, and, finally, the evil influence of Val Meeker had all contributed. But what Ladder had done Ladder must undo, and so Clem and his two helpers worked alongside of the grangers through the long, sweltering hours.

Brown and Yancey acted as though they might be going to balk when they came to Nat Brophy's fire-gutted homestead. Clem reined over to where the two cowhands had halted their broncs; swabbing his forehead with a sleeve while he fumbled for the makin's with his other hand, he told the pair: "I know what you're thinkin', about turnin' a hand to help the hombre that murdered Jap and Noah. It riles me too. But I've started this and I'm gonna go all the way.

"Ladder stock has no business bein' on Brophy's land. So come on, you two, and let's pull 'em off!"

Their looks were plain, but they didn't argue. Kicking up their tired broncs, they moved after Clem as he started in for the strayed Ladder steers.

Finally the whole job was done. Tom Peterson faced Clem with a deep scowl on his red face, and with words that had a hard time coming. "Ruby and the boys say we ought to thank you," he blurted. "I suppose they're right. But just the same, today don't change anything. We don't trust Hardins—that's the long and the short of it. You ain't workin' your way into our friendship with no gesture such as this one."

Young Hardin's tired, dust-streaked face looked old and bitter beyond his years. "I ain't biddin' for friendship, with you," he grunted. "Not after what happened out on the trail to Maxwell. I'm thinkin' of old Limp Kohler——"

"That was an accident!" broke in Ruby, the peacemaker "Luke Sands lost his head."

Clem shrugged. "The whole bunch of you was there. Reckon the sheriff will have to decide how much anybody was to blame. All I could do was make my report to Fox."

"Damn you, kid!" Peterson's voice shook with his rage. "I'm telling you right now—you better shut your mouth and keep it shut! Don't try and make trouble for us, or you'll turn up good and sorry!"

Clem returned the big Swede's angry scowl, not flinching. That strange feeling, of being older than time and sad with the wisdom of things, settled upon him again; he didn't feel at all brash, facing these grown men and talking back to them. He saw he had them worried, even if he was only a kid; that Peterson's loud talk was mostly bluster and that he as well as the others knew a real concern for what Hardin's testimony could do.

So he said calmly, "You and Chuck heard him, Talley. You're my witnesses with the sheriff that I was threatened. I want you both to remember just what Tom Peterson said."

"Right!" said Yancey. "It's writ in my skull with indelible pencil." Both punchers seemed to be enjoying the way the youngster was standing up to big Peterson and giving back better than he took.

"All right, then," said Clem, and his voice was tired. "Let's be getting back to headquarters. We're way overdue for grub."

He turned his sorrel, and the two punchers fell in beside him, bracketing his stirrup leathers. They left the farmers staring after them with dark and somber scowls. But Clem Hardin didn't look back.

At dinner in the kitchen, Brown and Yancey were boisterous with talk as they related to Shorty Jones the details of Clem's encounter with Peterson. The old cook seemed to enjoy it, but Hardin had little to say; a moody silence settled on him, for he was feeling again the nervous and physical exhaustion of the two preceding days.

He rose from the table tiredly when he was finished, and told his little crew, "I ain't got any orders for the rest of the day. I want to do some diggin' in the office safe and see what I can learn about the bank situation and the last tally count." It sounded kind of foolish, he thought, that he should know so very little about the ranch after living on it all his life. But it hadn't seemed like a part of him these last years since Jap and Noah took control. It seemed to him now that he had merely been marking time, drifting aimlessly through wasted days, waiting for his life to take some clear direction.

Shorty followed him from the kitchen. "I'm takin' the buckboard into town," he said. "Supplies we need. . . . Anything I could do for you while I'm there?"

Clem tried to consider, but his mind was empty of thought and he shook his head. "Nothin', I guess. Thanks, Shorty."

The cook hesitated a moment. "About them two hands," he said briefly. "Maybe I was a little previous. Looks like they'll do, after all."

"I think so," Clement agreed. "Chuck and Talley are all right."

"Yeah . . . Just forget I said what I did about 'em, will you?"

Clement went into the cubbyhole, dark and musty-smelling, that had served his brothers and their father before them as an office. There was a battered roll-top, a box safe that was never locked, a brass spittoon and a couple of chairs, and a deer head on the wall above the desk. It put a very odd feeling inside him to be entering this room as boss of the Ladder brand, closing the door and running the shade to the top of its roller—he had always hated the gloom of the place—and settling himself into the caboose chair which the broad, heavy frames of the other Hardins had filled before him. Responsibility had never weighed so solidly upon him as at that moment, and he sat there staring at nothing for a long time before he pulled himself together with a sigh, wheeled toward the box safe to drag open the sagging door, bring out a jumbled mess of papers, account sheets, and tally books. and pile them on the scarred desk before him.

Through the long hours of afternoon he grubbed through these books and papers, and he came out of the session with a crick in the neck and with eyes bloodshot from the unfamiliar concentration on cramped lines of figures. He pushed the mess of stuff away from him finally and, rising, went to the window where the bare hill behind the ranch buildings showed golden yellow under the dying day. He stood looking out at it, rubbing his stiff neck and hoping the unaccustomed eyestrain wouldn't give him a headache.

As little as he knew about bookwork, the picture shaped up clearly enough both for good and bad. Ladder had a balance in the Tilden bank, with only one small note whose installments could be met as long as beef prices stayed at a decent level. The tally sheets showed a good spring calf crop, a very fair book count in two- and three-year-old stuff. But there, in fact, was the danger. It was too large a count to be supported by a range going dry. Ladder would either need to find a new source to replace the forbidden water gaps on Kettle Creek or it must thin down its herds, pull in and wait for a turn in the cycle of wet and dry years. Disheartening, but it looked as though the latter would have to be it. . . .

Shorty Jones rolled into the yard on the seat of the ranch buckboard, its box containing bags and crates of canned goods from the general mercantile in town. The cook saw Clem at the open window and he braked his team, swung down, and came pegging over. He took the battered corncob out of his mouth, scowled at the fire-blackened bowl. "Uh—ran into Doc Warn in town," he announced shortly. "He wanted to know about the funeral. I said I figured ten o'clock tomorrow would be all right with you."

"Good lord!" Clem exclaimed. "I should of seen to that, but somehow I forgot all about it."

The cook said, "Well, bein' right there, I talked to the minister; he said he'd say some words for Jap and Noah and also arrange about the flowers." He hesitated. "I kind of took things on myself, I reckon, but I said you'd want to have Limp Kohler put away at the same time, him being a special friend of yours, and that you'd take care of the expenses. I hope you don't mind——"

"You know I don't!" Clem shook his head a little. "You saw I wouldn't be getting around to all that, and you took the job over without saying a word. I bet that was the real reason you went in today, wasn't it?"

His look was almost accusing. Shorty glanced away, shrugged, jerked at an ear lobe. "Oh well," he said vaguely, "I had some chores that needed doing——"

"All right, if you don't want to talk about it," said Clem. "But I guess you savvy I appreciate it. Well, we'll all be in town tomorrow morning, then."

He had been rather dreading showing himself there. But the time had to come eventually, and there was no use putting it off.

9

I T WAS a Saturday, when nearly everybody managed to get into town on some chore or other. Clem took his little crew with him—a solemn knot of riders, turned silent by the nature of their mission, and neatly dressed for the occasion in the best clothing they could turn out of their duffel bags. Clem himself wore a town suit he had had in the closet for two or three years; it was shiny across the knees and elbows and the seat of the pants, and its sleeves came inches short of the youngster's big, knobby wrists. But it was appropriately dark, and the nearest thing to formal buryin' clothing he owned.

Despite Shorty's obvious disapproval, he left his gun and holster at the ranch. "You don't wear firearms to a funeral," he said. "And I don't want anyone to get the idea I'm spoiling for a fight. Because I ain't."

"What if you run afoul of Meeker?"

Clem said, "I'll try not to."

There were horses racked in front of the Green Parrot, and a movement of Saturday customers across the veranda, but these were all farmers and punchers from the outfits south of Kettle Creek. No sign of Val Meeker or his tough crew——This put considerable relief in Clem; apparently they had pulled out of town, and he knew a hope that they might have gone for good.

Coming on into town, he felt something tighten up within him. The streets were alive with activity, and at every hand he saw curious stares turned on him, openly or furtively. Their weight was a real discomfort that made him stiffen in saddle and ride through the traffic of the dusty streets with fist balled tight upon the reins, young face scowling straight ahead of him. When he swung down in front of the minister's white-painted house, some scattered words from the lips of a passer-by reached his ears; he caught the name "Mart Raines," and knew that everyone in town must have heard all about the happening at Pringle's two nights ago. It had set tongues wagging for fair. He wondered what the gossips were trying to make him into, with their garbled talk. Some kind of a gun-slick killer——

Jap and Noah Hardin were laid to their final rest at ten o'clock, in a ceremony that was almost crude in its simplicity. A wagon and team hauled their pine-box coffins up the dusty road to the hilltop east of town and Tilden's thinly populated cemetery. Another hack followed, carrying Limp Kohler's remains, and then a small procession in buggies and on horseback.

Only a handful gathered around the open graves to hear the minister's empty phrases and see the first clods fall. The Hardins hadn't been too popular in life, and there was something so keenly horrible about their passing that the people of Tilden town seemed not to want to let it touch them, to contaminate themselves by attending these final rites. The grangers of Kettle Creek were, of course, noticeably absent. And Clem Hardin wouldn't have wanted them there.

As he turned away finally, dragging on his hat, he found himself suddenly face to face with Sally Fox and her mother. The marshal's wife put a work-worn hand on Clem's arm, gave him a warm look of quiet understanding. Sally Fox had some flowers in her arms. She nodded a little and said quietly, "Hello, Clem."

He said clumsily, "Thanks for coming." And added, "How's Bob?"

Mrs. Fox answered. "He's doing fine, Clem, though awfully weak. Doc Warn says he can be up in another day

or two, but of course he'll have to use a crutch until the
bullet hole in his leg mends completely. He'll soon be
right as rain again."

"I'm mighty glad."

He started to edge away, but she stopped him. "We
want you to come to dinner with us, Clem."

The boy colored a little. "Thanks, Miz Fox! But—make
it some other time, maybe?"

"Please, Clem!" said Sally. Her mother added. "We
planned on it. And Bob wants to see you."

"I'm sorry," he mumbled. "There's—there's a lot of
things waitin' for me at Ladder. I'll look in on Bob one
of these days, when I can. There's nothing I could tell
him that he don't already know——" He clutched his hatbrim and with a few more stammered words made his
hastry retreat to where the sorrel was rein-tied to the
graveyard fence.

It had been an ignominious scene, but he wasn't ready
yet to face these good people and the ordeal of their questions. Much of the confidence engendered in him by the
shooting at Pringle's had worn itself out since then. And
the fact remained that he had failed Bob Fox and owed
the marshal a full report to augment and complete the
hasty account he'd given in that scribbled note two nights
ago. At the moment he simply couldn't summon the nerve
to meet Bob's probing glance and fill in the details. He
took refuge, instead, in flight. He tried not to imagine
what Sally and her mother were thinking as they watched
him jerk loose the reins and step stiffly into saddle.

His crew of three were already mounted and waiting
for him. Shorty Jones's eyes asked a question, but Clem
said only, "You boys can stay in town awhile if you want
to. But get back to the ranch early, because tomorrow
we're starting a big chore—one my brothers should have
been working at weeks ago instead of wasting time pick-

ing fights with their neighbors. We're beginning our gather for fall shipment—and high time we did, too."

Chuck Yancey said, "I understood your brothers were holding out for higher beef prices later in the season."

"Well, we don't wait any longer. We've got to take some of the load off our range and our water supply pronto. Throw in everything that's marketable. Thin the stock down until it's more in line with the range we've got to feed them."

Talley Brown looked dubious. "Need a bigger crew for a job like that."

"I know," Clem agreed. "I'll see what I can do about raising one."

Shorty Jones, who hadn't said anything up to then, put in a sudden observation as their bunched horses moved off the cemetery hill and turned into one of Tilden's shaded side streets: "Tom Peterson—going into the marshal's place!"

His youthful boss glimpsed the big Swede's powerful figure swinging up the path to the neat cottage. For long minutes afterward he was frowning over this, wishing he knew what business the granger leader wanted to take up with the lawman. He had a suspicion, somehow, that their talk would concern himself. . . .

Bob Fox, resting in an easy chair on the porch, eyed Peterson's approach sourly and had his own question about the farmer's coming. It was the first time he had seen the Swede since the jail raid, and he thought grimly, *It's about time you were gettin' around to lookin' me up!* The thought didn't put any pleasure on his somber face as Peterson came striding solidly up the broad steps.

Peterson must have read the meaning of the scowl, but he meant to disregard it. He said genially, "Well, Bob, how's the invalid?"

The marshal shrugged. "Fair," he answered shortly, and countered with a blunt question of his own: "How's Nat Brophy—and *where* is he?"

Affability froze up in the face of the Swede instantly. "I think you're accusin' me of something!" he grunted. He stood there squarely braced on his thick legs, heavy farmer's shoes placed wide apart, jaw thrust forward as he looked down at the seated man.

Bob Fox shifted a little against the cushions at his back. "I think you know what, too. So let's not beat around the bush, Tom. I don't like this any more than you do—but I'm asking to hear your version of what happened on the Maxwell trail night before last. Bein' laid up, I had to wait for you to come to me. Well, let's have it."

"All right!" grunted Peterson, anger beginning to pinch the edges of his florid face. "That's just what I come here for. I got reason to think there's been some wild charges made against me and some of my friends. I'm telling you right now, Bob Fox, not to get into this any deeper. Forget about it—or you're apt to wish you had!"

"A man was killed, and a prisoner was released from the custody of the law." Fox shook his head. "That ain't easy to forget, Tom. At least, not for me! I dunno how *you* feel about poor old Limp Kohler——"

"I'm sorry about that as anybody could be." Peterson's voice lifted a little. "Good lord, I ain't inhuman! But Limp's gettin' killed was one of those unforeseen accidents." He caught himself. "At least, I figure it was. Of course I wasn't there."

"You tryin' to deny it?" exclaimed Bob.

"Certainly I deny it! What's more, I'm remindin' you that you got no jurisdiction in the thing and you got no business messing in it."

"There's the sheriff. If I file a report, he'll have an investigator here to do the job."

Peterson shook his head. His voice had a veiled edge. "But you ain't gonna file a report! Think it through, and you'll see why. What would an investigation turn up, Bob?" he persisted. "Just this: that you turned Nat Brophy, unarmed, over to the very man whose brothers Nat had killed—the one man who had the biggest reason to want him dead. You sent those two alone on the trail into the hills, with nobody along to try and hold Clem Hardin off his victim except for an old, beat-up man half crippled with rheumatism——"

Something cold ran through Bob Fox; he sat up straighter and he said tightly, "What are you gettin' at?"

"Plain enough, ain't it? Hardin killed Nat for vengeance, and buried him somewhere in the hills. Limp Kohler tried to prevent it, and Hardin shot him too; brought his body in with a yarn he invented laying the blame on us Kettle Creek farmers."

"You expect me to believe any such a thing—that Clem Hardin would commit *murder?* Why, Limp Kohler and him was as close as any two could be!"

Peterson shrugged. "I'm talkin' about what this investigator from the sheriff's office is gonna believe. It's gonna look to him like you made an awful damn bad blunder! You'll be up to your neck in hot water, Bob!"

"But—but *Clem Hardin!* Anybody that's known the boy will testify that he couldn't possibly——" The marshal was obviously shaken.

Peterson shook his head, satisfaction in him as he saw this break in the lawman's armor. He rammed the blow home. "Why, the whole range knows what Clem Hardin did at Pringle's; how he stood up to Val Meeker's whole crew and beat Mart Raines to the draw, without batting an eye! *That's* what the sheriff's man will hear about!

That's the picture he'll get—of a smooth-cheeked, cold-blooded killer. Just add it all up, Bob, and see what you think the county would do to him. And to you too—don't forget about *that!*"

Bob Fox's bony hands were knotted hard on the arms of his chair. A long silence fell between the two men; then the wind went out of Bob Fox in a long breath, and a tiredness came into his body. He slumped noticeably.

Peterson smiled crookedly. "Naw, I don't think you're gonna tell the sheriff anything——"

"Get away from me!" Bob Fox gritted with unaccustomed ferocity; but there was defeat and tiredness in his voice too. "Damn you, Tom, I don't want to talk to you!"

He was staring grimly straight ahead of him, into the leaf-dappled dust of the street. Tom Peterson stood a moment looking down at the grizzled head of the lawman, mingled emotions in him. He knew he had won the argument, taking him past a very narrow corner; but on the other hand, he liked Marshal Fox and it wasn't pleasant to have to put this kind of pressure on him. He tried to form words, to smooth off some of the lawman's anger, but a couple of tries failed and he gave up. He turned away, went heavily down the steps and to his horse tied at the picket fence, lifted his solid frame into the saddle.

Sally and Mrs. Fox came rolling along in their buggy, returning from the funeral. Peterson nodded to them in passing and touched up his bronc, turned it out of the quiet side street and into the busy traffic of the cow town's main drag.

He had one further piece of business here in Tilden that would be scarcely more pleasant than that scene with the marshal. Kate Brophy had got word to him that she urgently wanted a talk, and he couldn't put it off any longer; but he certainly wasn't looking forward to the prospect.

Tom Peterson didn't like Nat Brophy's wife, for the simple reason that he was a man ten years married and resigned to the dull repetitions of domesticity. Kate disturbed him. There was a carnality about her which she seemed incapable of withholding from her most casual dealings with men, and in Tom Peterson it roused troubling instincts and vague desires that a man had best leave smothered under marital routine. So he had always avoided her, but this time he knew she had good reason to demand to see him. Reluctantly he pointed his bronc toward the small two-room shack, at the west skirt of the village, where Kate had been staying since moving to town from the fire-gutted homestead on Kettle Creek.

Juniper and pine came right to the edge of the buildings, where a lava spur blocked further growth of the town on this western side. The few houses here were scattered, mean-looking tar-paper shacks, dark in the fringe of trees. Tom Peterson reined in before Kate's, uncomfortable, and at once the door opened and the blond woman stood looking at him, hand on one hip.

She must have just returned from shopping, for she was dressed for the street in a cheap dress that seemed to Peterson a little too low-cut and that fit too snugly her rounded, full-breasted figure. Her lifeless yellow hair was carefully arranged, her face done in rice powder and scarlet lip paint. She said, not smiling, "Well! I wondered if you were ever going to show up. Come in?"

He didn't budge from the saddle; despite himself he felt the color rising in his thick neck, and this angered him. "No!" he answered, a little too vehemently, and added, "I mean, I got a lot of things to do and I can't stay but a minute. What'd you want to see me about?"

"You ought to know what I want," she retorted a bit icily. "I been roostin' here for two days without any kind of news. What about my husband?"

"I can't tell you anything," said Peterson. "I haven't heard a word, either from him or from Luke Sands. I figure Luke must be hiding out, himself, somewhere in the hills—remember, it was him that killed Limp Kohler, and he's likely scared to death of what the law will do about it. As for Nat, all I know is he took Limp Kohler's bullet in the head, and when we split up Luke was leadin' his horse."

Kate's cheeks were colorless beneath their paint. "You —figure he's dead by now?"

"How do you expect me to say?" the Swede grunted harshly. "If he was bad hurt as I took him to be, though, it don't look like Sands would be a helluva lot of help to him. Nat was a bloody-lookin' mess." Peterson lifted the reins, wanting to get away from there. "I'll sure let you know, Miz Brophy, soon as I hear word from either of them. Meanwhile, for the love of God keep quiet about this! I think I've got Bob Fox talked out of starting trouble, as long as it's my word against Clem Hardin's. But if anything should leak, it would be rough on us all."

She shrugged. "I can keep my mouth shut," she said harshly. "And I can handle that Hardin kid. He made some insinuations, and I put him in his place, all right."

Peterson showed quick alarm. "Better watch your step with him! That kid is a deep one—I don't care how young he is. And now that he has Ladder, he's a gent to reckon with. Don't underestimate him!"

He added, "Well, I got to be goin'." A furtive glance, as he pulled away from the shack, satisfied him that nobody had been watching; he would hate to have word get back to his wife that he had been seen leaving Kate Brophy's. He knew considerable relief when he had left the shack well behind.

Kate Brophy stood for a long time as he had left her, leaning in the doorway, the frown about her hard mouth and brow reflecting the sudden working of new thoughts which Tom Peterson's words had started in her head.

All these things happened of a Saturday—the day of the funeral in Tilden town. It was late Monday, just at dusk, when the incoming twice-weekly mail coach from the county seat ran into trouble in the hills, five miles short of destination.

There was a steeply timbered grade where the horses, tired from their run, had to break speed until they were pulling against the collars at a climbing walk before they reached the top. It was customary to rest them here before taking the descent on the townside, while the yahoo and the shotgun messenger enjoyed a smoke and the customers, if any, stepped down to stretch their legs. But with the change-over of the seasons, darkness had gained a few minutes on each day, and this was the first time that year that dusk had overtaken the coach at this particular point. It was gloomy in the smoky silence of the timber; the chill air washing down the slopes had a bite to it, and the three passengers showed no inclination to leave their seats. The whip fingered the lines, said to the man next to him, "Reckon we'll push on as quick as the broncs are ready. Gets dark damned early in the woods this time of year——"

The rifleshot ripped open the silence then, scorching a bullet past the heads of the driver and the guard and breaking startled cries from both of them. A voice in the timber said: "The Wells Fargo box, gents! Let's have it down here!"

On the other side of the road a second voice added, "Don't anybody try for a gun, either! There's more of us than there are of you, and I don't reckon you got light enough to find a target. But you skyline as nice as anything, up there on that box——"

"Okay! Okay!" the messenger yelled. "Hold off your triggers!"

The whip was busy enough, calming the teams that had been spooked by that rifle bullet. The passengers were not of the stuff of which heroes are made, and the guard knew bad odds when he ran up against them. He was already groping under him, dragging the heavy strongbox from the boot, balancing it on the edge of the seat before he shoved it over. It dumped heavily onto the stony shoulder of the road. "There it is," he said hoarsely.

"*Bueno!*" the first voice answered. "Now, start 'em running!"

With fear in his voice, the reins handler yelled up his team. The coach went rocketing down the dark slope, sliding dangerously back and forth between the blurring walls of timber. Derisive yells lifted from back there at the crest of the hill, but were quickly swallowed by distance and the noise of the careening stage.

The horses were still boogery when the coach rocked into Tilden and disgorged its frightened, voluble passengers. In a matter of minutes, news of the holdup had spread through town; for trouble on that loop of stage road was a thing almost without precedent. The story grew in size and horror as it snowballed from tongue to tongue; and sooner or later, of course, it reached the ears of Bob Fox, the marshal.

Old Bob heard the news, and his tired face went gaunt and hard. He looked at his informant, and then at the alarm in the eyes of his wife, who stood near by with a tray of food in her hands—Bob's supper, which she had been about to lay across his knees. Bob shook his head.

"Put it back in the oven," he said. "And get me my clothes. I've done my last sittin' with *this* skewered leg!"

"But, Bob!" cried his wife.

"I got things to do. And I ain't noways hungry—this

thing has plumb knocked the appetite out of me. Get my clothes, will you, and that crutch. Sally, I'll need the buggy . . ."

He had been practicing with the crutch and he could just manage to get around with it, despite the tenderness of a partially healed leg. When the buggy was hitched up, the old marshal's wife and eldest daughter helped him up onto the seat, not arguing, because they knew Bob had a stubbornness that couldn't be defeated. He put his crutch beside him, handy, and took the reins.

"But where are you going, Bob?" his wife pleaded, her veined hands knotted together anxiously.

"Don't worry about me!" he grunted, relenting a little. "I'm just gonna see a man or two. I ain't heading for danger. . . . Now, get those kids out from under the horses, will you?"

Sally herded her younger sisters out of the street and Bob flicked the reins, turned the buggy in the middle of the street, and headed it back toward the center of town.

He drove first to the stage station, and from there to a nearby eatshack where the driver and guard and the passengers were drinking hot coffee and trying to calm down enough to get some solid food into them. Bob managed to get the answers to the questions he put them, and pieced together something approximating the facts of what had happened out on the road. He learned that the station agent had already seen about sending word to the sheriff's office, and as it would be futile trying to lead a posse into the hills tonight—even if it had been in Bob's own jurisdiction or he had been well enough to sit a horse—there seemed nothing demanding action of him.

So he hoisted himself into the buggy again and rode directly to Ed Pringle's Green Parrot dive, just beyond the edge of town.

There were lights in the place and the mechanical

piano was making its racket; otherwise the saloon seemed pretty quiet. Bob put his horse to the tie pole, climbed down, and held onto the buggy for support as he pulled the crutch down after him. The rubber tip made a small thumping as Bob hitched up the steps, along the veranda, and pushed sideways through the swinging doors.

The Green Parrot was rather ornate, considering the sort of dive it was. It had a crystal chandelier and expensive layout of games, a long cherry-wood bar. There was even actually a parrot, chained to its perch beside the mechanical piano, where it prowled back and forth and squawked its choice collection of profanity.

Most of the games were closed now, with only a desultory poker game running at one of the tables back from the door. Ed Pringle stood at the bar, discussing some business matter with the bored tender. They looked around as Bob Fox stumped into the room, and an unreadable look quickly settled into the saloon owner's sallow features.

"Well, Marshal!" he grunted. "Don't remember ever seeing you in my place before. Sort of out of your bailiwick." He added that suggestively, reminding Fox that the town limits ran just the other side of the roadhouse; and then he ordered, pleasantly enough, "Set 'em up for the marshal, Spike."

Fox said, "No likker tonight, Pringle."

"It's on the house."

"Thanks just the same." Fox had a hold of the bar edge, easing his weight off the crutch to which he wasn't really accustomed yet. He was beginning to feel shaky already; this was the most work he had done since that bullet and the loss of blood had knocked him out of commission. At his age you didn't mend right away from a thing like that.

He said, "When did you last see Val Meeker?"

Pringle's hawkish features took on a hooded careful-
ness. "It must have been three, four days ago. Why? Any
particular reason?"

The jangling of the mechanical piano was a jarring
thing suddenly, because the room had gone motionless,
the men at the poker table turning to focus on the scene
at the bar, every other sound coming to an end. Even the
parrot seemed to notice something was wrong with the
atmosphere of the big room. But the piano ran on, mind-
lessly, working out the nickel somebody had dropped in
the slot.

Bob Fox had to talk into this strange blending of racket
and uneasy silence. "You must have heard by now," he
said, "that somebody lifted the Wells Fargo box off the
Maxwell stage this evening. With Val Meeker and his
gang running loose in the hills, it don't seem hard to me
to add up the answer!"

"You're guessing!" Pringle rapped. "I was under the
impression Meeker had pulled out."

"I think different! I figure he ain't had all he wants out
of this range and we'll hear plenty more from him before
he leaves us alone for good. I figure you know that too."
His mild eyes hardened. "You been pretty thick with
that crowd, Pringle. People are going to remember that,
should it be proved for sure that Meeker robbed the
stage!"

Ed Pringle's lean frame straightened with a jerk. "Are
you threatening me, you two-bit town officer?"

"Hold it!" grunted Bob. "And tell your aprons to take
his hands off that bar gun—I ain't wearing any." The
bartender flicked a look at his boss and carefully lifted
his hands above the edge of the counter. Fox went on, not
taking his eyes from Pringle's face.

"I'm not threatening anybody. Like you say, any authority I got don't hold this far north of the jail. But I

am warning you that folks here are getting a little fed up with this dive of yours—especially after the shooting here the other night. And if Meeker gets out of hand, that won't help you any either. You might even find yourself gettin' chased out of this country . . . or even given a ride out, on a rail! Just think it over, fellow."

Pringle's mouth twisted. He spat, "I don't find that talk very amusing. Get out of here, and take it with you!"

"Sure," said Bob blandly. "It's your house. But since you don't seem to know much of what goes on outside of it, I figured I ought to give you a little advice. I didn't hardly think you'd take it."

The wooden crutch made a small clatter against the bar as he reached for it, dragged it around into position, and got the pad under his arm. The piano battered out some final chords, whirred and stopped; and the silence was complete. Through it, Bob Fox hitched himself toward the door and shouldered through.

Despite Pringle's talk, Bob knew the man was worried. "I gave him something to chew on, all right," the marshal thought as he clumped back to this tied buggy, and he chuckled a little. "If he'd just scare bad enough to run, the range might get one benefit, anyway, out of this mess."

But, riding back to town, he quickly sobered again. The complications had been bad enough before, and they were getting worse. Tom Peterson and his grangers, aligned against that brave youngster on Ladder Ranch. Nat Brophy and Luke Sands, both turned killer and missing somewhere in the hills. And now Val Meeker and his bronco crew gone on the make for whatever they could grab for themselves. . . . Where in Tophet *would* it end?

10

THE slap of a six-gun jarred the morning stillness; the startling whine of its bullet ended in the thud of lead into a pine branch only yards to the right of Clem Hardin. He didn't wait for a second shot. As the echoes of the first smashed and rolled away through the wooded silence, he went bodily out of saddle, hit the pine needles that littered the dappled hillside, and sprawled there, full length, his heart trip-hammering. The sorrel danced ahead nervously, then halted and turned to look back at its fallen rider.

Clem did not move. A band of warmth across his shoulders warned him that he lay at least partially in the full glare of the sun; but this was an open space, only dappled by shade of the tree heads, and he had little chance of finding real cover. The best hope he had was to make his ambusher think the one bullet had done its chore.

Though he strained to hear, the only sounds he made out were the throb of his own pulse, in the ear that was pressed hard against the earth, and, somewhere off along the foothill slope, the shrill cries of a jay, fading as the bird threaded in flight through the trees. A faint wind whispered in the pines, and the sorrel blew and scraped a shod hoof through the rubble. Then the silence thickened, became almost complete.

Still Clem lay as he was, not daring yet to move. He tried to reconstruct the shot, from his fragmentary impressions of the startling moment; but he couldn't discover any clue pointing to its direction. When at last no

second bullet followed, and he felt something like a full
ten minutes must have gone by, Clem decided he had
lain there long enough.

He came up lunging sideward, jerking his own six-gun
and ready for the hidden gun to lash out again. Nothing
happened. Slowly, Clem let some of the tension run out
of him, convinced that the bushwhacker must have de-
parted after the single try. He didn't give over any of his
caution, however, or return the gun to his holster just
yet. He carried it in his hand as he walked forward, got
the trailing reins of his bronc, and stood a moment pon-
dering the meaning of the thing that had—almost—happened to him.

It could have been one of the grangers; it could have
been a member of Val Meeker's tough bunch. He didn't
try to go any further with his guessing. It was terrible
enough that a twenty-year-old youngster could so readily
name even that many potential enemies who might have
lain in wait to level him with an unseen bullet from the
brush. . . .

On foot, and leading the sorrel, Clem began to hunt
for sign. He knew only that the shot had come from somewhere ahead and to his left, and he swung a widening
semicircle across this upward slope, patiently searching
the needle-littered earth. He found little evidence; thick
pine needles don't take a trail, and only in one open
spot of soft earth did he locate a couple of prints of a
shod horse. They seemed to point toward the ridge above
him, so he swung to saddle and made for there over the
steep and slippery needle carpet.

Other pine-clothed ridges stretched beyond its crest,
building higher toward the backbone of the mountain
range. An antelope feeding in a park below him broke
and made for the underbrush. There was no other move-

ment, and Clem knew that any further search for the bushwhacker would be futile.

His pulse had slowed to normal, with the passing of danger; he sat saddle for a long moment, resting and dragging the sweet, resin-scented breath of the pines into his lungs. The tang of distant smoke had left the air, he noted. The fires must have burnt themselves out, back in the hills.

Clem Hardin was tired. It seemed he never got enough rest any more, and there had been no letup in the nervous strain which was as physically exhausting as any labor. This was the third day of the gather which Ladder had commenced prior to fall shipment and the thinning out of his herds. It was a terrific job, indeed, for three men—Shorty Jones being too badly used up for saddle-work. You needed a full-size crew for such a project; but, as Clem had feared, riders were not to be had. He would keep trying, of course; meanwhile the work had to be done, in some way or other, handicapped though he was.

And so, pulling the sorrel back, he took the descent of the ridge again and left the business of the ambusher where it lay—an unsolved mystery, pointing to the dangerous tension which lay across Ladder graze, and the enemies who would stoop to any means to be rid of its young owner.

He jumped four head of cattle grazing the thin growth in a glade and put the sorrel at them, worked his coiled saddle rope and got the critters lumbering ahead of him toward the flats. Down there in small, three-sided natural pockets which hastily built fences had converted into pens capable of holding fifty head or so apiece, Clem and Brown and Yancey were throwing their slow gather.

Later, after catching any branding jobs that had been missed in the spring, they would push all these smaller holdings into a low-walled basin where the entire gather could be held with little trouble by a few riders. If he could round up a trail crew by that time, Clem would then make his drive to the rails at Maxwell; otherwise he would have to make a dicker with a cattle buyer for range delivery. It was certainly none too soon for Ladder to begin thinning out its beef. The grass was almost gone, the water alarmingly low. The grangers along Kettle Creek, having remended their fences, were keeping a constant and suspicious guard on them. Clem Hardin had no illusions that any deal could be made with Peterson and his friends. He got the plain impression that they would like to see Ladder broken on the cross of a dry year and go down without any helping hand from its neighbors. And less than an hour ago Clem Hardin had been shot at from ambush—as likely, as not, by one of the Kettle Creek farmers themselves. . . .

Chuck Yancey had just finished shoving some strays into one of the brush-fence pens as Clem showed up; he lent a hand chousing the latter's gather in with the others, whooping and slapping them in with a shapeless hat. They got the gate swung to and fastened; a steady lowing came from the shifting mass of red-and-white shapes within the pen. Yancey ran a sleeve across his face, swabbing sweat and caked dust from it. He said, "Damn, it's hot! I though summer was supposed to be over about now."

"If the rains ever start, it'll turn cold fast enough." Clem slanted a worried frown at the sky, deep and unbroken blue above the piny ridges to westward. No clouds up there around the glistening peaks, or even a haze of any kind. "I dunno why they're holding off this way."

He had made up his mind not to say anything to his crew about the ambush attempt. It wouldn't do any good, and it might work harm with their morale, which was running a little thin of late anyway. Shorty Jones was steadfast as ever, but after all, Chuck Yancey and Talley Brown were little better than drifters, and this thing was beginning to look pretty big to them. Spending hours in saddle pushing recalcitrant stock out of the hill breaks and into the pens—and then spending other hours on a wagon seat, hauling water to them—this endless labor could take the strength and the spirit out of a man. Clem's failure to find other riders willing to sign on and lighten the work had been the thing which started his pair of helpers to grumbling.

But at the moment Chuck Yancey seemed to have forgotten his grievances. Hearing an exclamation from the man, Clem looked at him quickly and saw a lopsided grin building in his broad, stubbled face, a gleam in his eyes as he looked at something past his boss. "Well I'll be damned," he chuckled. "Look what us polecats has got for company!"

Turning in saddle, Clem Hardin saw, and his jaw almost dropped from astonishment. Kate Brophy was the last person he would ever have expected to see on Ladder range—and certainly not such a Kate as this. She rode sidesaddle on a sleek livery-barn pony, a trim ankle just showing beneath the edge of her wine-red skirt. Her blouse was a frilly one, snugly fitted to the bold contours of bosom and waist. She carried a ribboned parasol slanted over one shoulder, shading her from the harshness of the high sunlight; her yellow hair was piled carefully, with a pair of curls like pine shavings dangling beneath her left ear. As she saw Clem looking at her, too-red lips broke into a smile.

Chuck Yancey groaned in mock distress. "Oh, you chicken!"

"Shut up!" Clem muttered, coloring.

Then the woman was in speaking distance and she

called pleasantly, "Hello, Mr. Hardin. I bet you're surprised to see me, aren't you? Your cook told me I'd most likely find you here, somewhere."

As Clem was fumbling for words, the man beside him cussed a little, good-naturedly. Just loud enough for Clem to hear, he said, "Looks like my cue to beat it. Well, watch your step—'*Mister* Hardin.'" With a grin and a broad wink he hauled his cayuse aside and touched it up with the spurs, gone before Clem could make an answer. A moment later Kate was beside him, pulling in, lowering her parasol as she smiled at the youthful Ladder boss.

"My!" she exclaimed, chattering amiably. "When I started out for a ride this morning I didn't know I was gonna be gone so long. Feels like this damn saddle has plumb left its mark on me." She smiled again, sweetly, as though innocent of anything out of the way in her remarks. "Won't you give me a hand down, Mr. Hardin?"

The last time he had laid eyes on this woman she had spat venom at him and given him the flat of her hand across his face in a whack that still ached in retrospect. Now she was all simpering charm and helpless femininity, and he couldn't any way explain the startling change in her.

Acutely uncomfortable, he came down from saddle and moved over to her horse, reaching up clumsily to take her. She leaned, put her hands upon his shoulders; she was pretty heavy, considering, and when he lifted her down he did it awkwardly and her body came against him, in a swirl of skirts against his legs and a cloying wave of perfume that was an irritant to a nose more attuned to the smells of horse sweat and saddle leather. Red of face, Clem set her on her feet, but for a moment Kate Brophy was close to him, her painted lips curving up at him, her hands still on his shoulders.

"My, you're strong!" she murmured. And then, with a throaty laugh, she turned away, flirting the cover of her parasol open and shut a time or two and tucking it under an arm.

Poor Clement was totally at a loss. He might have understood what was going on here had he been less ignorant of women or could he have read the thoughts working beneath Kate Brophy's bleached blond head.

For Kate was thinking, *This poor damned simp! To think I'd wind up doing an act for a kid out of the eighth grade!* But none of these feelings touched the surface of her, for Kate was playing to big stakes. Youngster or not, Clement Hardin was the heir to the Ladder brand —a—ranch that lacked only water to return it to its former importance as a cattle empire. And the Brophy homestead, bordering on Ladder, would give access once more to Kettle Creek and the water Clem's range had to have. This fact was Kate's hole card, which she meant to play for a killing. A lease of some kind to the Brophy water rights—maybe even a partnership; these were possible, of course, but not good enough for Kate when, by handling her cards adroitly, she might end up with Ladder itself.

And Clem Hardin was so plain stupid and wet-eared that it didn't seem to her possible she could play her hand wrong.

She looked up at him roguishly. "You're wondering what I could be doing here, ain't you?"

"That's the truth!" he admitted.

"And I don't blame you. The fact is, I'm just damned ashamed of myself, and I felt I had to come and apologize for the way I've behaved. I'm afraid I ain't been very— neighborly."

"That shouldn't worry you none," he answered curtly. "Neither have the rest of my neighbors!"

"But it's not right!" she insisted. "You didn't start the

trouble. And after what my husband did, you tried to help us—tried your best to keep him from gettin' killed. Wasn't your fault if you failed."

Clem looked up. "You figure Nat Brophy's dead, then?"

"I can't figure otherwise. I'd of heard—he's had time to get in touch with me, somehow or other. I—I guess he was bad hurt, all right. And out in the hills, without any help except for that no-good Luke Sands——"

"Guess you're right," he admitted. And added, before he thought, "Too bad. He ought to have hung!"

He started to wince, half expecting that hand to come raking across his face again. But Kate Brophy didn't even look angry. Instead she turned and put a hand on his arm suddenly, gripping his sleeve. "He should!" she agreed fiercely. "Maybe it don't sound right for me to say this, but it's the truth and I can say it now. I stood by Nat while he was alive because I was his wife, and, mainly, because—I was afraid of him!"

"Afraid?" he echoed, the incongruity of the thing jarring the word out of him. "Afraid of Nat Brophy?"

"Oh, you just don't *know!* He was a beast, Mr. Hardin! Sometimes, the way he'd carry on—the tempers he'd fly into, the horrible things he'd say for no reason at all —I used to think he must be more'n half crazy. Sometimes I've wanted to run away from him, but I couldn't! I didn't dare! He might of done to me what he finally did to—to your brothers!"

Clem couldn't doubt the sincerity of this. There was real, naked fear in her eyes. "I always figured Brophy for a queer kind of duck, but—doggone if I dreamed it was anything like that!"

"Nobody did!" she insisted. "You think I'd married him in the first place, if I'd of guessed? He come to that place in Boise where I was—uh—entertaining. He was drunk and blowin' his money, makin' a lot of talk about how big-time he was, about the size of the spread he owned out here on Kettle Creek. Well, what was I to think—a poor girl, workin' for a living? I thought he was telling the truth. I thought he was a—a gentleman!" Her reddened lips twisted bitterly. "I let him marry me, and bring me back to that two-bit homestead, and threaten me with beatings and worse if I ever dared to leave it! It—it was just plain hell!"

He frowned, looking down at her solemnly. "You should have asked for help, Miz Brophy. If it was bad as that."

"But I didn't dare! I tell you. I was scared for my life; I knew he was crazy enough that if he found out I'd said anything——"

"Why, I'm plumb sorry!"

Clem Hardin meant it. In that moment he felt a great pity for this woman, in the plain anguish of her poured-out story. His words were poor enough, but they seemed to have effect. Kate Brophy's look changed subtly; the remembered terror went out of it, was replaced by a new expression—something vaguely seductive. Her fingers, laid upon his arm, were suddenly caressing.

"You ain't like—him," she murmured. "You're real good, Clem. You wouldn't hurt a woman that loved you and was—nice to you."

All at once Clem got it. Burning to the ears, he stumbled away from her—from this woman with the bleached hair, the painted face already hinting of middle age, who had laid her feeble trap for a youngster years her junior. He muttered hoarsely, "If you mean what I think you do, ma'am, you're wasting a heck of a lot of wind."

He saw her eyes change, saw the fury flash into them; then this was veiled, and she dropped the lifted hand that he had winced away from and stood looking at him with the beginnings of a thin smile quirking her lips.

For Kate saw then that she had gone too far and moved too fast, and that Clement Hardin was at once both smarter and even more naïve than she had thought him.

For a moment neither spoke, and the lowing of the cattle in the pen came across the stillness that stood between them. Then, with a lifting of her shoulders, Kate Brophy turned abruptly and went straight back to her waiting pony. She looked over her shoulder at Clem. "Well?" she said mildly. "Are you still a gentleman, or not?"

With a groan, Clem strode forward, offered a palm for her foot, and almost pitched her into the saddle. He stood silent and glaring while she carefully arranged the wine-red skirt, smoothed its folds across her knee. She held out her hand. "The reins, please—*Mister* Hardin?"

Clem got them and handed them to her. Her eyes still held his face, with an unreadable amusement. She shook her head a little. "You're making a mistake," she said. "Even if you don't want me, I got something you need— the way to save Ladder."

"Thanks!" he gritted. "I'll save it my own way!"

She only smiled. Suddenly she lifted a hand and touched his cheek with it, playfully. "You know, you're kind of cute when you're peeved." And before he could pull away from the caress she was turning her pony, with a mocking laugh, and spurring away from him—a woman thwarted in this first try to get what she wanted, but obviously not yet ready to cry "Quits!"

Cold fury in him, Clem Hardin stood and watched her ride away. Then another sound caught his ear, and he heeled about quickly. For the first time he spotted the rider who sat a grassy ridge a couple of hundred yards away—a small, denimed figure in the saddle of a buckskin mare. Even as he looked, the buckskin whirled and started away down the farther slope, at the hard jerk of its reins;

the rider, head thrown high and shoulders squared, was sending it away from there as fast as the buckskin could be made to travel.

Clem stood and yelled, "Hey! *Hey, Sally!*" Then, belatedly, he turned and ran to his own sorrel, threw himself into leather, drove the bronc right at that grassy ridge.

Topping it, he saw Sally's mare laying a funnel of dust as the girl pressed the buckskin hard, not looking back—not even when Clem, in sick desperation, yelled her name again. His jaw clamped then, and he leaned forward in the saddle and set the spurs. The sorrel slid down the slick, burnt slope, stretched out. And quickly, as the brown grass blurred beneath his sorrel's pounding hoofs, the distance between them was quickly cut down.

Once Sally looked back and Clem saw her face, white and set in angry lines. "Please wait!" he begged, above the noise of their horses. But with a toss of her head she had straightened around again, not faltering.

Clem's sorrel had some of the lines of a quarter horse; on a short run it could outmatch an ordinary bronc, and in his determination to make Sally pull in and talk to him, Clem dug out everything the sorrel could give him now. Slowly he drew up on the buckskin; Sally saw him gaining and tried desperately to whip up speed with her rein ends. But then, leaning from saddle, the youngster had a grip on the bridle, and in another moment both broncs had pulled to a stop, dust building about them and whipping away in the faint breeze. Sally cried furiously, "You just let go of my bridle, Clem Hardin!"

"I won't!" he said, tight-lipped. "You've got to wait and let me explain."

"No. I'm not in the least interested; it's nothing to me if you let that awful female paw you. Like—like she was trying to *reduce* you," Salley raged, groping for a word and not quite finding the right one. Her alleged indifference did not wear well in the light of the tears glistening and trembling in her eyes.

"But, Sally!" he begged in despair. "I tell you it wasn't —we didn't—Oh, I don't even want to talk about it!"

"I bet you don't!" she said grimly. "And neither do I!" Her voice choked. "I wish I'd never come out here today! I wouldn't have, except Dad asked me to."

"What did Bob want?" demanded Clem, grasping at a new topic for conversation.

She sniffed, recognizing the subterfuge; but she answered, "He thought you should be warned—about Val Meeker's gang. They held up the Maxwell stage last night and took the Wells Fargo box—or did you maybe know about it?"

"No!" exclaimed Clem. "I didn't."

"At least, Pop thinks it was them. And he knows you've got a couple of that crowd working for you, and he wanted me to find out for sure that they couldn't have had anything to do with the holdup."

Clem said, "Chuck and Talley? Oh no! They was in the bunkhouse; I can tell you that for a fact. Besides, they never were a part of Meeker's gang."

"They helped in the raid on the jail, didn't they?"

"Yeah, but that time they were drunk. They come back to work when they'd sobered up, and I'll vouch for it they haven't had any contact with Meeker since then— not for at least five days, anyway." He shook his head. "No, they're nothing but a pair of saddle tramps—no better an' no worse than that. You don't need to worry about them."

"*I'm* not worried," she retorted, freezing up again. "Why should I be? I'm sure it's none of *my* business what goes on out here at Ladder. . . . Now, will you please let go of that bridle?"

"Aw, Sally!" cried Clem. But he did as he was told,

and he sat helplessly and watched the girl turn her bronc without another look or word and ride away from him, her young, strong body stiffly erect in saddle. He watched while she dwindled in size and then disappeared into the willows lining a dry, mud-caked watercourse. As soon as she was out of sight he began to think of the things he should have said; but by then, of course, it was much too late.

A dead weight of hopelessness settled inside the boy. This seemed the worst morning he had lived through yet, all the things that had happened to him. What more was there left to happen?

11

H E LEARNED the answer to *that* question not more than thirty hours later, when Talley Brown, with a great air of foreboding, took him to witness the evidence of what had taken place at one of the little holding pens at the edge of the hills. The brush fence had been torn down, the hollow was empty of the cattle that had been pushed into it at the expense of weary hours in saddle for Clem and his two helpers.

"Eighty head in there yesterday," said Brown. "From the sign, I'd figure no more'n two men did this—and it must have been recent; maybe three hours past. A damn lot of nerve, cleaning 'em out in broad daylight!"

A kind of fury seized Clem Hardin. He was no expert at reading sign, but the story was plain enough and no effort had been made to conceal it. The trail of stolen stock pointed straight toward the near hills, and the prints of two shod horses were clear enough. As Brown had said, this thing couldn't have happened more than a couple hours ago—likely as not, some time since noon.

"Let's get goin'!" grunted the youngster, looking up to the piny slopes stretching toward the snows. Here, at least, was a foe you could strike at, throw a physical weight against; it gave almost a welcome relief after the events of yesterday—the attack by an unseen ambusher, the agonizing scenes with Kate Brophy and Sally Fox. A consuming desire to take after the men who had lifted his stock shoved aside caution for the moment.

But Talley Brown hung back. "Maybe we better have help," he suggested hesitantly. Clem whirled on him.

"And give them time to lose us in the hills?" he demanded. "The trail's fresh, but it won't stay that way long. If you're scared to come with me, I'll trail alone, damn it!"

The puncher's lean face went white; he said angrily, "You ain't callin' me no coward!" And without another word he spurred past Clem and was already started on the torn-up track of the stolen cattle before his young boss could get under way.

Clem kicked his bronc forward, quickly overtaking the man. He said, "I'm sorry, fellow. Guess my temper's running kind of thin. Don't mind anything I say."

Brown shrugged a little. It was the only comment he would offer; when he spoke again, twenty minutes later, it was to make some irrelevant observation about the trail they were following.

This presented no problems; the sign was completely fresh and easily readable, as though the cattle thieves expected no trouble or were even contemptuous of anything Ladder might do in rebuttal. Clem suspected the latter of being the true explanation, and it put a dark anger inside him.

Did everyone take him for an utter fool, gullible and unable to look after his own interests?

He rode hard, setting a stiff pace across the steepening slants of the mountain foothill ranges. His bronc was the chestnut bay he had killed Mart Raines over—a mount with bottom and sturdy legs for climbing. Talley Brown, on a lighter mount, had to keep pressing to keep up, but he didn't make any complaint, despite Clem's blindness to the danger of wearing out the other bronc. Clem seemed like one possessed, and Brown didn't appear

anxious to invite another lashing of the youngster's un-
reasoning temper.

Pushing like this, and not encumbered by driving
stock, they knew they must be steadily gaining on their
quarry. An hour went by unnoticed, and another. The
ranks of spruce and pine wheeled overhead and fell back
against a sky that turned an ever-deeper blue as the afternoon grew old. The tangy scent of the needles was sweet
as a bronc shouldered past an occasional low-jutting
branch and its rider lifted an arm to ward it from his
face. Neither rider spoke much, for there were few dif-
ficulties of the trail to be discussed and ironed out between them, and the increasingly harder travel discour-
aged talk.

Presently, however, they came through a fringe of thinning timber, and a gently sloping bench opened ahead of
them, with a row of autumn-tinted cottonwoods lining a
moss-thick stream. Where the hoofs of the stolen cattle
had torn the margin of this rivulet stirring mud that had
not yet completely settled, Tally Brown suddenly pointed
out a thing that Clem's own inspection confirmed.

"They met somebody here," said Brown, "and par-
leyed while the cattle drank and grazed a spell. Then they
went on with the cattle and the third gent rode off alone
—that direction." He pointed on a tangent into the trees,
where shadows were already starting to lengthen as the
sun lowered toward the westward peaks.

Clem nodded agreement, his young face bleak. "I'll
take one guess as to who that third gent was, giving them
their orders."

"Meeker?"

Not bothering to answer what seemed a perfectly obvious conjecture, Clem Hardin considered the further
trail of the stolen beef as it crossed the stream and pointed
at a slant northward into the timber. "Where do you

think they're aiming to get rid of that meat? They must have some ready market in mind for it."

"There's wildcat logging operations goin' on across the mountains," Brown suggested. "And a railroad's going through the valley. They'd be able to peddle meat, all right, and no embarrassing questions likely."

Clem nodded. "That's it, then! They aim to take 'em across Washrup Pass, clean up what they can get, and bring the cash back to Meeker. So they'll make camp somewhere this side, tonight, and take the pass come morning." He flicked the reins impatiently. "They can't be too far ahead right now. We should catch up to 'em easy before nightfall."

Dusk came early, though, at that season and in the shadow of those high mountain ranges. It descended upon the pair of riders, and it lay like blue smoke among the trees and thickened each moment, until the uneven and rocky terrain took on a treacherous danger and pine bole and manzanita clump, lava boulder and deadfall, became increasingly dim impediments to travel. The moon was up, but its light did not reach far into the tangled darkness of the pine-roofed steeps.

Talley Brown reined in finally. "We can't go much farther," he grunted.

"We got to," said Clement, frowning ahead through the gathering night that was chill with the altitude and the lateness of the year. "Come morning, they'll be across Washrup and we'll never catch up with them."

"It's ridin' blind," the puncher objected. "Eighty head of cattle been through here before us, but that still don't make it a trail that's a cinch to follow."

"When the moon gets higher——" And then Clem Hardin broke in upon himself. "Wait! *Listen!*"

Speech died as they sat saddles, listening for a repetition of the sound Clem thought he had heard. For a long minute there wasn't anything but the wash of wind in the pines overhead—a steady susurration that blanketed other night noises. Clem began to doubt his own senses. Under him, the bay shifted footing restlessly and saddle leather made a sharp popping. Standing in stirrups, the young Ladder boss was testing every movement of the chilling air, beginning to think his senses must have tricked him.

Brown said sourly, "I'm listenin'——"

And at that instant a shifting of the wind brought from straight ahead of them the faint but definite bawling of a steer.

"And I'm hearin'!" the puncher completed his sentence gruffly. At once the pair of them lifted reins and were moving forward, a tingling of excitement mounting in Clem until it seemed enough to choke him. Or perhaps it was fear he felt. He knew only that a trembling was in the hand that fisted the reins.

They skirted the spur of a ridge and in thinning trees pulled up sharply. Filtered moonlight showed them a small meadow, protected by the shouldering hills; they saw faintly the stir of the grazing cattle there, heard the murmur of a rivulet. And, not far from the mouth of the grassy pocket, a jewel of flame made dancing shadows. A campfire.

Without a word, both Ladder men came down from saddle and snubbed reins to a sapling pine, and then moved forward cautiously to the very edge of the timber growth where they could get an unobstructed view. "Two of 'em, all right," Brown whispered after a moment's silent inspection of the camp layout.

The rivulet made its sound not far from the camp spot. The leap of the flames threw wavering shadows of the two who moved about it and crouched beside the fire, evidently putting together a bait of trail grub. Their

horses ranged beyond, on pickets, and between the rust-
lers and the grazing cattle farther back within the pocket.
The broncs still had their saddles, because it might be
necessary to use them again before the beef stock was
definitely settled for the night.

Brown said, "Those jokers don't suspect there's anyone
within miles. If we can just take advantage of that and
surprise 'em——"

"We'll take them from two sides," said Clem. "You stay
in the timber and move up from this direction. I'll make
a circle. We'll move in as close as we can without revealin'
ourselves."

The other nodded his agreement with this plan. Clem
Hardin slipped the six-gun from his holster, checked it,
and went silently forward, doubling over as he left the
protection of the trees.

The moon was not too strong here, and the brightness
of the fire would help blind the unsuspecting pair yonder to movement beyond the circle of the camp. Never-
theless, it was no easy thing to move out upon the open
meadow, with no better cover than the long, reedy marsh
grass that carpeted the dark flat. But the plan was his
own suggestion and he would not go back. Talley Brown
had already struck off through the trees and brush, carrying out his own part of the arrangement.

He discovered quickly that the ground underfoot was
none too solid; the rivulet, spreading and dividing, had
turned it into a marshy bog, and as he prowled forward
over squashy mud and moss, cold moisture began to work
in through the stitching of his boots. He found himself
hampered and slowed down by this, and once he slipped
and went down in the water, stabbing a hand into the
mud to steady himself, the gun in his other fist hastily
drawn up to keep it from getting wet. He stayed like that
a long, breathless moment, eyes lifted toward the fire to

detect any sign that the men there had noticed the splash his falling had made. If they had, they seemed not to be paying any attention to it.

Clem went ahead. He was close enough now to make out the faces of the pair, and they were certainly Val Meeker's men. They still did not appear at all aware of the danger moving up on them; Clem wondered if they would let themselves be taken without a fight, and he hoped they would. He found himself hoping it with an intense fervor. This thing had him jumpy. He was scared, and he knew it. . . .

And then everything went wrong.

The sound of a dead branch breaking cut like an explosion above the murmur of the stream. The men at the fire jerked around toward the noise—and there was Talley Brown's figure, dimly visible in fireglow where the snapping of the deadfall branch had caught him. At once the pair of cattle thieves, prodded by the startling sight, were pawing for holster leather.

Talley Brown shot, his gun flaring redly. The guns of both men answered him. What was to have been a trap had broken wide apart, with its victims opening fire before they had had a chance to see they were whipsawed. Clem Hardin heard himself yelling, found himself running forward, slipping and scrambling in the marsh bog that clung to his feet and held him back. He cried, "Hold it! Hold it!" and brought his own weapon forward for a snap shot as he ran.

At this moment one of the pair went reeling, a shout of pain tearing from him as he dropped his gun, grabbing at his gun arm with his other hand. Talley Brown had got over a good shot. And now Clem Hardin snapped the hammer of his gun and a bullet drilled past the head of the second man, so close that the outlaw yelped and ducked way from it. Trying to come about to face this new danger, he caught a spur in some weeds and stumbled, went down heavily on all fours. Then Clement was running into the fireglow, his gun trained dead center on the man, and shouting, "Let it go! Don't try it, Walters!"

His warning took effect. Walters saw the uselessness of further fight; he crouched there on hands and knees, not moving, as Clem came up and set one muddy foot on the outlaw's gun. Clem said harshly, "Leggo of it and climb onto your feet."

As quick as that the fight was ended. Tally Brown strode up to the fire, apparently unhurt in the sharp, fierce exchange. Bud Tiehman, the other outlaw, was on his knees, doubled over his hurt arm and slobbering with pain. He was wailing, over and over, "You smashed it! Damn you, you smashed my wrist!"

"Shut up a minute, can't you?" growled Brown. He looked at Clem. "What do you want done with them?"

Hardin frowned uncertainly. He didn't know what to say; it was a question he hadn't considered during all the long hours of trailing this pair.

Somehow he hadn't thought of them as turning out to be men that he had known personally. But of course Bud Tiehman and Jed Walters had ridden for Ladder, along with the rest of Meeker's bunch; Clem had rubbed elbows with them at the same table, had taken their veiled hoorawing when he was the youngest Hardin and the one nobody paid any great attention to. Now the turns of circumstance had put them on opposite sides of the fence, and his decision would say whether they would take the punishment they had coming, as stock thieves caught red-handed with their stolen Ladder steers.

He remembered, too, that Marshal Fox held these men guilty of the Maxwell stage holdup; but that wasn't proved. And after all, these were the small fry of Val

Meeker's outfit. These were the sheep who followed Meeker's orders—though dangerous enough sheep withal. And Tiehman, for one, wouldn't be harming anybody for some time to come—not with a broken gun wrist.

Clem thought all these things and then he shrugged heavily. "We'll turn them loose," he said, "after they've helped us take these cattle back to where they stole them from. We'll let them take a message to Val Meeker—tell him the next time his men try to trim Ladder, maybe we won't be as lenient!"

Tally Brown was scowling at him. "I don't like it! Cut down the odds while we got a chance, I say. You gonna give Meeker the idea we've gone soft or something!"

"No," replied Clem firmly. "We're turning them loose. Go get our broncs, will you? We'll tie this pair up, make use of their camp tonight, and trail back in the morning. Maybe you better take a look at the cattle and see for sure the gunplay didn't get them rattled."

"All right," the puncher growled with poor grace. "You're the boss!" But his lean face showed a scowl as he heeled about and strode away to follow his orders.

Suddenly tired, Clem let himself down with his back against a chunk of lava rock. He waggled his drawn gun at Walters. "Try what you can do for your friend's arm," he said. "But watch yourself."

He sat there, hungry but too tired yet to move to help himself to the outlaws' food supply. He listened to the groans of the hurt man, the crackle of the fire, the sounds of the rivulet and of the grazing stock, and of Talley Brown riding back to camp with Clem's horse trailing at the reins. He felt that the main thing he wanted right now was to go to sleep. . . .

Trailing those eighty head back to Ladder next morning, Clem rode high in stirrups with an eye not only on the stock but also for possible trouble from Val Meeker, whom they might encounter anywhere in these hills. But there was no sign of him, nor did the two prisoners offer any trouble. Sullenly, they followed orders and helped shove the stolen bunch eastward, retracing the course of yesterday, keeping them bunched and holding them from scattering in the timber. Bud Tiehman, with his broken arm, was not much help; he complained continually of the pain and the crude job of emergency bandaging that had been effected with a torn-up shirt and with clean, straight pine sticks for splints. It was about all he could do to stay in saddle, sagging to the jolt of his bronc, largely blind to everything about him.

When at last the steers had been returned to their pen and the brush gate fastened against them, Clem Hardin turned to face the sullen pair of prisoners. He said, "You two have given us a lot of trouble, and I got every reason to turn you in; better be thankful I ain't going to." He added, "Where's their guns, Brown?"

The puncher came up with them. He had shaken the cartridges out of them, and he rode round behind the pair, shoving the weapons into their empty holsters. As he returned Tiehman's he grunted, "You won't be needin' *yours* for a spell—that's certain." Reining clear, he gave Clem a final displeased warning. "I still think you're making a bad mistake, boss."

Ignoring him, Clem told the pair: "Get riding!"

For the first time in a couple of hours Jed Walters spoke up then; he showed no particular gratefulness for being offered his freedom. He said, "You think you're pretty damn cute, I reckon. You think maybe you'll have Val Meeker scared stiff now?"

Clem shrugged. "Just tell him he better keep his hands off Ladder beef after this. That's all I'm interested in."

"We'll tell him!" the outlaw promised darkly. He jerked reins and spurred away into the timber, the hurt

Tiehman trailing him. Clem waited until both were out of sight and then he nodded to the scowling Talley Brown. "We better get back to the ranch. Shorty and Chuck will be wondering what happened to us since yesterday, and I reckon those guys won't make another play for this particular bunch of cattle—not with Tiehman put out of commission."

Brown didn't say anything; his whole attitude spoke a strong disapproval of Clem's handling of the thing and dire forebodings as to the future. Young Hardin himself was doing some serious thinking. Prompted by the re-entry of Val Meeker into the picture, he was beginning to see that his plans were going to need sharp revising; and by the time they reached Ladder he believed he saw what his decision would have to be.

At ranch headquarters they found Shorty Jones as worried as a mother over the prolonged absence of his young boss. He had to hear the entire story as he went to work throwing together some food for the hungry men who had not eaten since early morning. Chuck Yancey was out somewhere, riding range. The two dusty, unshaven riders ate off the oilcloth-covered table, the old cook hovering over them and listening grimly to Clem's terse recital.

Building a smoke above the remnants of his meal, Hardin said finally, "How many head you figure we got collected at the various holding points, Talley?"

"Maybe eight or nine hundred."

Clem shook his head. "That's how I figure it—and it's not enough. But maybe we'll have to be satisfied with it."

Shorty Jones put in, "My rheumatism's been pretty good these last few days. Bet I could fill a saddle again if'n I had a bronc wasn't too peppery under me."

The young Ladder boss looked up at him with a smile above the match flame shielded in his hard brown hands. "Nothing doing," he said. "You got a man-size job to do,

without trying to kill yourself." He shook out the match.
"No, we're gonna have to cut short the gather. It's too
much of a temptation for Val Meeker, leaving our cattle
scattered around in little bunches for his men to pick
off at their leisure. Starting tomorrow, we'll pull them
all in together, throw them in that big hollow at Sandy
Springs——"

"And then?" prodded Talley Brown dubiously.

"Why, we'll hold them there until I've found extra
riders to help us make a drive. I'll go clear to Maxwell,
if I have to, to locate trail hands."

Brown said, "You won't find 'em! News travels fast;
every saddlepounder driftin' across the grass will have
heard by now that Val Meeker has got this ranch marked
off for his own pickings, and they'll stay clear like it's
poison."

"Then I'll deal for range delivery. Surely I can find a
cattle buyer who ain't scared to bring his own men in
and drive off the herd."

"You'd stand to take a bad loss that way," Shorty
Jones protested.

"Can't be helped." Clem pushed up from the table
tiredly. "I've figured all the angles and I come out with
only one thing sure—that I ain't in any position to make
terms! This here is about as close to a lone-handed fight
as any man ever faced—let alone a half-growed kid, which
is all I am." He ran a big-knuckled hand through tawny
hair. "Dunno where I'd be if it weren't for the loyalty of
you three ranahans."

"Well, you've got that, anyway!" Shorty Jones assured
him with fierce intensity. Talley Brown, staring sourly before him at the littered oilcloth, made no comment at all.

12

The day Clem rode to Maxwell, Shorty Jones gave him tense warning before he pulled away from the ranch: "Watch out for Meeker, y'hear me, trailin' through them hills!" But neither then nor on his return trip the following afternoon did his wary caution discover any sign of the outlaw or his men.

In the sleepy county-seat town he heard barroom talk of the trouble on Kettle Creek—of the stage robbery; of Val Meeker's going on the loose and his attack against the Tilden jail; of the murder of the Hardin brothers and the mysterious vanishing of their killer. Garbled stories floated freely in Maxwell, and when Clem recognized or identified himself as the last of the Hardins, and owner of the Ladder iron which was so deeply entangled in all these sinister events, he saw how men backed away from him quickly, as though his troubles might somehow prove contagious.

He tried to approach a couple of chuck-line-riding cowhands who trailed in about the time he arrived, with sougans strapped down behind the high cantles of their stock saddles. His offer of a riding job was met by hostile, suspicious stares and a hasty turndown. They wouldn't even let him buy them a drink—a rare thing indeed for a chuck-line rider. They didn't want the disaster of which he was a center to touch them in any way.

If he had wanted to contact the sheriff's office he couldn't have done it, because neither Joe Lawrence nor his deputy were in town that week. Having met rebuff and a chilling fear of involvement everywhere he turned, he went at last to the telegraph office at the railway depot. He sent a wire off, had lunch at an eatshack across the tracks from the station while he waited for an answer. The reply, when it came, necessitated a second wire to clear up and settle some points as to prices and terms. By the time a swollen, reddish ball of sun was hanging low in the smoky mists across the valley, he had made his arrangement for range delivery of the nine-hundred-odd Ladder steers which were even now being held and guarded in the rocky basin on Hardin range.

The terms were none too advantageous, but Clem had no experience in driving bargains and he had everything —including the pressure of time—against him. Feeling he had accomplished the best that could be expected under the circumstances, he folded and pocketed the yellow telegrams and went to get his chestnut bay out of the public stable where he had left it. It was already close to night-fall, but he began his homeward trek, making camp by the trail under the murmuring yellow pines, and mounting in early dawn to push on again through the hills.

Trailing back to Ladder ranch, he by-passed Tilden town; since that dismal encounter of a few days ago with Kate Brophy and Sally Fox, he had seen neither of them and he didn't want to see them now. He didn't know what he would ever find to say. He rode wide of such a meeting, crossing Kettle Creek at a rocky point above the granger homesteads where the farmers were keeping jealous guard now on their gleaming wire. He came to Ladder headquarters toward late afternoon—and was filled with a quick alarm at sight of the horses tied to corral barns and veranda railing.

Among the rest he marked a black gelding which he knew instantly belonged to Val Meeker.

He kicked his tired bronc forward quickly under the high gateway. He was a hundred yards from the big, sprawling house when someone shouted warning, and at once men came into view, moving out through the front door. He caught the glint of a rifle barrel in the shadow of the veranda, and would have hauled rein but for a terse warning that rapped across the intervening distance: "Just keep coming, fellow. We got this pot-wrangler of yours up here in case you feel inclined to be difficult."

Shorty Jones's sour voice confirmed the warning. "Yeah —company, Clem. They got guns. Being all alone, there wasn't much I could do about it."

They had brought their hostage out onto the veranda, to show Hardin the danger of any rash move. Unwilling to place a risk on Shorty's safety, he rode on obediently to the house, where he stepped down from saddle in a dead silence, ground-hitching the bay. Jed Walters, who had the rifle, said, "Right up the steps and inside. Val's waitin'."

There was a kind of unreality about it all, mounting the sagging steps under the stare of those watching, hostile eyes. As he started through the door he heard Jed Walters say, "Wait a minute," and felt the gun plucked roughly from his holster and then replaced—but with the handle reversed, so that it jutted forward in an impossible position for drawing, even had Clem been foolhardy enough to consider trying it. Walters gave it a shove deep into the leather, making sure it would stick there in event of a hasty pull. "Okay," he grunted. "Right on in."

Four men were in the room—only a half of Meeker's gang. Bud Tiehman's bandaged arm was white in the semidarkness of drawn curtains at the window. Yonder, Val Meeker's solid frame filled a big, leather-slung chair behind the center table; his boots were up on the edge of the table, and the spurs had scraped a deep gouge across its surface. He looked up with a mocking grin on his dark features, taking Clem's measure in a slow, insolent survey of the boy's long length. It was the first time these two had met since the Ladder's ex-foreman had slogged Clem Hardin into unconsciousness with his fists and boots, that fateful day of the murder of Jap and Noah.

"How long this bunch been here?" Clem demanded of old Shorty, speaking across his shoulder while his eyes bored into Meeker's. The outlaw gave the answer.

"We only rode in a few minutes ago. Jones said you was gone to Maxwell and wouldn't be back today. You trailed in just as we was fixin' to leave—almost missed us."

"What do you want?"

Meeker had a broken spur strap in his hands and was toying with it, twirling it, running it idly through his hands as he considered the boy's trail-tired face and dusty clothing. His mouth beneath the roached black mustache twisted in a slow smile that did nothing to warm his eyes. He said, "Why, I told you we'd be comin' back one of these times. We got thirty days' back pay each comin' from you—remember? We need the cash."

Shorty Jones gave a snort, somewhere behind Clem. "Wasn't enough in that Wells Fargo box to hold you a spell?"

Nobody paid the slightest attention to him. Val Meeker was watching Clem with a hawkish intensity, and the boy found a stubbornness hardening inside him as he returned that cruel stare. "You stole Ladder beef," he replied flatly. "That cancels any debt there might have been. I don't owe you hellions nothing and I ain't payin'."

Val Meeker considered this, without any apparent anger. He waggled his boots on the edge of the table, looking at the dusty toes with that same secret amusement. The audacity of Clem's defiance did not seem to bother him.

He took his feet down then, set them solidly on the floor, and pushed up from the deeps of the big chair. "Sound pretty sure of yourself," he muttered. "I don't see what reason you got to feel that way—unless it's because a couple of the boys were careless and let you take a handful of steers away from them. Could that be it?"

Clem didn't answer. He stood his ground, with enemies at either hand and unseen behind his back, and faced Val Meeker as the outlaw came to him around the table, halted a scant two feet away. Meeker's voice began to take an edge; anger began to color his eyes. "Well, speak up! You tryin' to act like you ain't scared?" His hand flipped up suddenly, struck a sharp, open-palmed blow across Clem's face. "Answer me!"

A trickle of blood started from the corner of Clem's lower lip. He touched it with his tongue. Face white, he said slowly, doggedly, "I ain't afraid of you!"

Meeker let out a grunt, his brow dragging down a little. He seemed to be finding a core of resistance in this youngster he hadn't expected to find; he couldn't read the stubborn, fatalistic pride which was all that really carried Clement Hardin in that terrible moment.

Then his face went impassive, a hard scorn taking shape upon the man's flat lips. "All right—you punk kid! I'm gonna show you what respect I got for you and for this Ladder spread. I'll just make you a little bet—hell, no! a *promise!* I know you're holdin' something short of a thousand head of stuff out on your range. I figure they're worth takin'. And tonight . . ." He paused, letting the thing build up before he finished. "Tonight we're gonna come and run off the whole bunch of them! You understand me? I'm *tellin'* you, right to your face—I'm givin' you notice in advance. What's more, I'm sayin' that, even so, you won't be able to do a damn thing, when the time comes, to stop us! Is that puttin' it plain enough?"

Clem didn't try to answer for a minute, as he let the bold warning sink in. The amazing audacity of Meeker's boast had him stopped. He tried to pick the thing apart, to read in it some hint of the man's thoughts, the source of his confidence. But Hardin's brain seemed a wooden fumbling thing just then, as he stood there with that dark gimlet stare cutting into him.

"Well, what the hell!" somebody snorted. "Can't the guy say anything?"

Hardin dragged in a long breath. "You can come ahead," he said in a leaden voice. "We'll be lookin' for you!"

"Then look mighty hard!" grunted Meeker, and he sniggered. "I got an idea you'll see more than you want to of us!"

Abruptly, he had turned away with a jerk of his head at the men who had come here to Ladder with him, and now boots tramped the hard wood floor as his gang followed him outside, the interview quickly ended. Clem stayed just as he was, staring at the wall, his big hands clenched tight; he didn't look around, didn't turn to the window as the quick thud of hoofs took Meeker's quickly mounted crew streaming past it in a boiling dust. He didn't move until he heard Shorty Jones bleat an angry curse and make a dive for the mantelpiece where a long rifle rested on pegs beneath a shaggy buffalo head.

"Damn 'em!" the old cook screeched. "I'll send 'em off with——"

Clem lifted his head, said sharply, "Let it alone, Shorty! Let 'em go! You hear me?"

"But—but——" Incoherent with rage, Shorty whirled on him; but he left the rifle where it was. "What the hell we gonna do about that wolf pack, son?"

"Nothin'. Right now, we do nothin' at all. But we'll try and be ready for them when they come tonight!"

The old cook came to him, scowling darkly. "You think he meant it, then? You think even Val Meeker would do anything as crazy as to raid us after warnin' us he was comin'?" His voice was husky with incredulity.

Clem nodded. "That's exactly what I do figure. Meeker don't make idle talk. He's gonna raid that herd all right —and he feels doggone sure he can get away with it. He came here just to tell me that, and to taunt me with it. But if it's the last thing I do, I'm gonna see to it he turns out mistaken!"

The sudden firmness of his voice must have told old Shorty Jones that Clem's mind was set, a determination reached inside him that wasn't to be shaken. The old cook started to tremble all at once, with excitement and with dread.

"If this is to be showdown with that hellion crew," he declared hoarsely, "then so let it be. But there ain't much time to spend gettin' ready for 'em. Somebody best head for town; few friends as Ladder has got, there still ought to be some who'll back her hand! I'll hitch up the buckboard and ride in myself; maybe I can make folks listen to reason——"

"No, Shorty!" Clem had the old man's arm, halting him as he would have headed toward the door. He shook his head, and saw consternation and unbelief wash across the face of the old cook. "We're not yelling for help! This is Ladder's fight."

"But just four of us!" Shorty croaked. "Against no telling how large an outfit Meeker may have collected by now! You gone outta your head? You like the idea of committin' suicide?"

Clem looked at him. "I'm not askin' you to walk into a thing that don't make sense to you," he said quietly. "But lemme tell you what I got in mind, before you decide. You know that hollow where the shippin' herd is; you savvy how the sides are ringed with rock, with only the two ends open. Looks to me that four determined men, with saddle guns and plenty of ammunition, could hole up in the rocks commanding those two entrances and keep out an army!"

The old man looked suddenly thoughtful, seeing the picture. "You could be right," he admitted slowly. "Though, if there was gunfire, wouldn't it be apt to stampede the cattle?"

"How could it? If the steers spook, the racket will just drive them deeper into the hollow. Or, if they did charge one of the openings, we'd be in position to drop the leaders and drive the others back."

His argument carried weight. He began to see a gleam of rising excitement in Shorty's faded eyes. "You know, damned if you ain't right! Four men—why, boy, play our cards right and they couldn't hope to knock us out of those rocks, or get to the cattle either, no matter how many of 'em come after us! I got to hand it to you! It just shows the advantage of plannin' a war on your own ground!"

"Maybe." Somehow Clem Hardin couldn't avoid a feeling that he had missed something—that there must be some factor he'd overlooked. Meeker was a clever and unscrupulous man. He wouldn't lay all his cards out on the table the way he had just now, face up, without holding at least one or two of the high trumps up his sleeve. . . . Yet, try as he might, Clem could not discover any element that he hadn't taken into consideration. It baffled him—and filled him with vague misgivings that contrasted strangely with the enthusiasm his plan had kindled in the old pot-wrangler.

Well, the chips were down. He lifted his shoulders heavily. He was tired from the long trail back from Maxwell, and now a nervous tension was already making itself felt within him at the thought of what might be coming in a very few hours from now.

He realized that Shorty was asking him a question—something about the two-day trip to the county seat. He wanted to know what the outcome had been, and Clem told him briefly about the deal he had made by wire. "If we can hold these steers, the buyer and his crew will be here in five days to pick them up," he finished. Shorty didn't like the terms that had been agreed on; but after all, if you didn't have men enough on the pay roll to move a herd yourself—— He nodded gloomy agreement.

"Time to start thinking about food," Clem said then, returning brusquely to the situation just ahead. "Better stew up an extra gallon of coffee, for tonight—we may have a long siege ahead of us and it's gonna be chilly. I noticed a haze building out of the west that looked like it might cloud up on us."

Shorty jerked around and hurried to a window. "You don't suppose," he exclaimed, squinting at the sky, "you don't suppose we're gonna get us a *rain?* It's been so long I wouldn't know any if I saw it!"

"I ain't making any bets," said Clem. "Right now, I got to get out to the herd and let Chuck and Talley in on what's stirring tonight—give 'em their chance to pull out if they don't feel like facing this business. After all, they got nothing at stake—just their own lives."

"Yeah," grunted Shorty. "Let them drifters pull out right now if they're scared of a fight. The two of us can hold that pocket alone, if we have to. We'll throw so much lead at them hellions of Meeker's they won't know where it's all comin' from!"

"Two could do it, maybe," Clem admitted dubiously. "But four could do twice as good a job. . . . But it's up to them. I ain't asking anybody to risk their neck for me unless they figure it's worth it to check a varmint like Meeker."

He went out to his tired and dusty bronc, made a quick switch of gear onto the fresh sorrel, and headed out toward the hollow, three miles northwest of the ranch headquarters, where his two riders were keeping an eye on the shipping herd for him. The afternoon was dragging out, and with its waning the haze he had been watching in the west was taking more definite shape, thickening and spreading. Above the piny ridges an edge of cloud sheet showed now. A chilly breeze came before it, cutting like a knife blade through the warmth of brassy sunlight. Clem thought it was really beginning to look as though it could rain.

In the broad and grassy hollow where the herd grazed peacefully, they would have protection from the worst of any weather; the raw, rock-sided walls would serve as a windbreak—and they had so served many a gather of Ladder beef stock in years past. Now, riding in through the near entrance, Clem found the cattle feeding undisturbed; and Talley Brown and Chuck Yancey came spurring to meet him.

Yancey, he saw, had a livid bruise along one side of his

wide jaw. He said, "Well, what happened to you, Chuck? No doors out here to run into, are there?"

The puncher colored a little, and lean Talley Brown, hoorawing him, said, "The damn fool was looking at his bronc's hind hoof to see if they was a stone under the shoe. Bronc hauled off and kicked him—couldn't pass up a temptation like that, I reckon."

Clem laughed, but Chuck didn't seem in a mood to be amused at such remarks. He cut in with a blunt question. "What luck in Maxwell? Hire any riders?"

"No," said Clem, sobering. He added, "Let's light down and talk a minute, fellows. I got some news for you—and something you're gonna have to decide for yourselves. Not much time to talk it over."

They went down and squatted with their backs against a rock face where the warm sun lay upon them, and Clem told the pair everything, not pulling any punches. They listened soberly; neither had any questions to ask, and when he was finished the youngster said into the silence, "I wouldn't want anybody walking into a thing like this unawares. I need you both, for what's certain sure to happen tonight. But I couldn't blame you if you want to draw your time right now and pull out of it." He pushed to his feet. "Just think it over; I won't press you for an answer."

The two looked at each other. Clem went to his horse and was fumbling for stirrup when Talley Brown spoke. "We've already decided," he grunted. "It's a losin' proposition, but I reckon we'll be around when the fun starts."

Clem wanted to thank them, but the two wouldn't even look at him as they went back to their own horses, swung into leather, and reined away toward the grazing herd. He called after them, "Shorty will bring grub with him. We'll be out here before dark, and get set for our visitors." And then he spurred back toward headquarters as the advancing cloud sheet slid across a westering sun, and the colors went out of things, and a premature hint of darkness came with the strengthened chilly wind that moaned across the brown range.

This season of unnatural heat seemed on the verge of breaking, sure enough; rain would bring with it a new hope for Ladder—if Ladder itself could weather the more dangerous storm which was due to break before another dawn showed above the wide horizon.

13

I<small>T</small> was close to nightfall when he left headquarters again, to ride and join his three-man crew. Shorty Jones had already gone, driving his buckboard with boilers of hot grub and coffee steaming in the back of it. Clem pulled the house door shut, went down the veranda steps toting a heavy windbreaker, against the chill of the coming darkness, and his saddle gun in a leather scabbard. With fingers numb from growing tension he fastened this in place, and was lashing the coat behind the cantle when sound of a horse in the dust lifted his head abruptly. He hadn't even heard the buckskin approach, but there it was; and Sally Fox sat saddle looking down at him, alarm building in her eyes.

"Clem! What on earth——"

He said, "I thought you weren't speaking to me any more."

Sally made a gesture. "Can't you forget that? I was mad that day. I—I never really meant the things I said. I knew there couldn't be anything between you and—and that ——"

"All right," said Clem shortly. "It's forgotten." He fiddled with the lashings of the saddle strings. This was one time when he just didn't have it in him to talk to Sally, or anyone else. The shadows were lengthening; time ran fast and he needed to be elsewhere.

The tense impatience must have shown in his manner, because Sally was saying, "What's wrong, Clem? There's —there's something afoot; I can tell from the way you're acting! I've had the funniest feeling all day, as though something told me you were in trouble. It got so strong that I had to come——"

Clem tried to make light of this. "It's right kind of you, worrying about me. But there's no call to—nothin's wrong." Yet he himself could tell that his voice was tightening up in his throat; it didn't sound natural to his own ears. Then he saw the girl's troubled stare drop to the wooden rifle stock jutting from the leather scabbard. He saw the startled shock that gave her.

"Clem Hardin, you're lying!" she cried. "I've never seen you with a saddle gun before. What are you going to do with it?"

"Why, there's a loafer been cutting down some of the young stock on the north range," he told her, thinking quickly and coming up with what seemed to him a good explanation. "I'm going out tonight to see if I can spot him."

She didn't believe him. She was looking about her now, at the dark and deserted buildings. "Where's your crew?" she demanded. "And Shorty! Even he—— Oh, Clem, why can't you be honest?" A choking that sounded very much like a sob cut into the steadiness of her speech.

"You won't believe nothing I tell you," he grunted gruffly. "What's the use of telling you anything?" He stabbed a boot into stirrup, lifted into the saddle. "I thought you was different from that, Sally!"

"Well, you see now that I'm not!" Suddenly the tears were there, blinding and unheeded. "If you love a person you're bound to worry about 'em——" Then, as she realized what she had blurted, color began at her cheeks and slowly flooded through all her face, clear to the open collar of her shirt. "I didn't mean to say that!" she cried. Her mouth began to tremble. "And now that you know, you'll make fun of me!"

"Gosh, Sally! I'd—I'd never do *that!*" Clem Hardin felt

something working in his throat; for a moment he thought he was almost on the verge of crying himself. He was emotionally tied in knots anyway, without having this thrown at him unprepared.

Not that it was really so surprising. He had known for a long time that Sally liked him, perhaps in a special kind of way. But he'd always thought of her as so mature and certain of herself—so more or less grown up, though in actual point of time the girl was some two years younger than Clem. Somehow it seemed incredible to think of her as being in love with such an overgrown, hopeless youngster. Not bright, sweet Sally——

If they hadn't both been on horseback he might have tried to kiss her then, but instead he fumbled for her hand, squeezed it awkwardly. And after that, because the pressure of tonight's events was too great and time was rushing ahead too fast for his mind to rest long on any other subject, he said, "I got to ride now, Sally. Don't worry about me—please! Everything will be all right."

He was gone then, at a quick gallop. And Sally Fox watched him through a haze of tears until he was swallowed from sight in the gentle slopes and swells of the land, and the spreading shadows.

Misery was a heavy thing in the heart just then, coupled with a kind of relief at having unburdened herself of a secret that had been hard to bottle up all these months of her love for Clement Hardin. But at that moment all other feelings were swamped in a dreadful certainty that the fears which had brought her out here to Ladder were too well founded. Clem's manner and his hasty departure had spoken volumes. She knew where he was headed, too. She knew about the good-sized bunch of cattle Ladder was holding in a hollow up that way. Something must have threatened them. And what could that something be, except—Val Meeker!

Yes, Clem might have been dismayed to know just how little he had managed to conceal from that girl!

She didn't try to follow him. She turned her buckskin, instead, and rode away at a lagging gait along the town trail, since she knew there was nothing she could do to help. Most likely she would just succeed in getting in the way. She was only a girl, after all.

But there must be *something!* She thought of her father. Bob Fox certainly would have done anything in his power to get out there and lend a hand; but he was only half recovered from the weakness caused by his skewered leg, and he couldn't walk yet without the crutch. No, he couldn't help much. There were others, however, who were perfectly capable of fighting—men who should be *made* to fight, if they had any neighborly decency in them, or even a selfish desire to get the cloud of Val Meeker's lawlessness lifted from this range of theirs——

Suddenly she knew what she was going to do. It settled in her and found a stubborn core of strength which was part of her heritage from the fine old man who was her father. With eyes still red from that brief flurry of tears, but with firm young jaw clamped hard and shaped by determination, Sally kicked her pony forward into a new burst of speed. Whatever might be due to happen this evening, time was obviously growing very short.

The buckskin was stretched out at a dead run when she came into the yard of a homestead layout not far from the murmuring banks of Kettle Creek. The pound of hoofs brought a man hurrying from the barn, holding a lantern against the gathering gloom. Sally pulled up, not missing the look of utter astonishment revealed in his heavy features by the wash of light from the lantern.

"Tom Peterson," she told him bluntly, "I want to talk to you!" And she *was* talking, before he could do more than stammer out an uncompleted question. . . .

The night was turning out really cold—cold enough to make Clem Hardin plenty glad of his impulse to bring a sheepskin windbreaker along with him. He hunched down into its protection, his rifle resting ready to his hand against a flat-topped boulder just in front of him. The six-gun was in its sheath, under the tail of the coat; but a moment's warning was all he would need to flip the coat aside, get the weapon into his fingers. There was plenty of ammunition for both the guns.

His three-man crew were all equally well equipped, and they had chosen positions commanding the two entrances to the hollow and protected from attack from any side. The more he considered it, the more unlikely it seemed to Clem that Meeker could hope to knock them out, even with vastly superior forces, and so get at the herd—it would be too risky an effort, hardly worth the losses it surely would involve. And yet Meeker had made his brag, and it hadn't been an idle one. Young Hardin couldn't free himself of the nagging conviction that he must have overlooked something, must have left some vulnerable chink in his armor, and that Val Meeker was aware of this and would know just where to make his thrust when the moment came.

Plagued by this uneasiness, the boy crouched in his rock hole-up and looked out over the hollow—a formless black gut in the moonless darkness. Those clouds had pulled across the sky, sweeping steadily in, and they made a canopy admitting no leakage of starshine. Beneath its pressing roof the wind blew steadily now, rattling the branches of scrub growth and sage, moaning in crevices of rock, putting a numbness into Clem's red-whipped cheeks. Staring into the dark, he could make out the dim and shifting pattern of cattle in the hollow, the darker bulk of the opposite wall, where Shorty Jones, he knew, was likewise waiting out the cold and dragging hours.

When would the danger strike, and where?

He moved, shifting cramped, cold limbs. He found himself remembering that scene an hour ago with Sally Fox—her blurted confession, and his inadequate reply. He found himself thinking, *She couldn't have known what she was talkin' about. She couldn't really feel that way about me——* All his doubts, his misgivings about himself were mounting high within him. In the crisis that lay ahead of him, how would he acquit himself? How would he demonstrate his right to be called a man, and no longer a green youngster whom circumstances had shoved against a problem too big for him? . . .

Movement in the shadows of the slope came to him, suddenly. He heard the definite sounds of a boot crunching stone, of thorny brush tearing as it caught at the clothing of a body moving through it. Gone clumsy with quick excitement, Clem lifted to his feet; he put his hand on the cold barrel of the canted rifle, then instead reached for the gun at his hip, pawing aside the coat to fumble for the wooden grips. Dimly he thought he could make out now the shape of a man against the shadowed rocks.

A voice called softly, "Where you at, boss?"

With the gun half pulled from leather, Clem hesitated. "Who is it?" he demanded.

"This is Talley Brown."

Clem recognized the voice this time. Relaxing, he said, "It's a dang good thing you spoke up. I was about to start shooting. . . . Come on in."

The puncher scrambled across the slick stones, slid in behind the rock barricade beside his boss. Clem could hear his breathing but could hardly see him in the starless gloom. Brown said, "Gettin' colder!"

"Yeah." Anxiety touched Clem Hardin. "What made

you leave your position, fellow? We don't know when they might start the fireworks."

"No sign of 'em yet," said Brown gruffly. "And there's something I gotta tell you."

Clem shrugged, shoved the gun back into holster, pulled the sheepskin tighter against the chill. "Well?" he prompted. "What is it?"

"This!" Something hard rammed against Clem's side. On a harshly altered tone the man grunted, "Put up your hands! Lift 'em high!"

For the first horrible moment Clem Hardin couldn't comprehend what was happening. Head jerking around, he tried to read a meaning in the face of the man, but it was no more than a dim blob in the night. He stammered something, a question that broke short after the first word or two; for then the truth dawned horribly on him and he saw the shape of the treachery which must have been Val Meeker's hole card—the one flaw in his armor that Clem had overlooked.

"I said, *'Lift 'em!'* "

The gun barrel bored deeper, painful despite the thickness of the sheepskin. Slowly, Clem's hands lifted. But at the last moment, turned desperate, he was twisting suddenly and making a wild grab for the rifle leaning against the boulder in front of him. He felt the cold metal of it brush his fingertips—and then a clubbed forearm drove into his face, driving him back and down. Landing heavily, he heard the rifle go clattering before a kick of Brown's boot toe; and after that Brown was leaping full upon him, with a weight that knocked the breath from him.

The six-gun was jerked from his holster. The chill touch of a gun muzzle was laid against his face and Talley Brown's hoarse voice said, "One more funny move and I'll kill you, Hardin!"

He got to his feet slowly, still holding the gun against Clem's face. He ordered, "Get up!" The youngster lay there for a long moment, however, fighting to get air back into his lungs. His belly felt sore where the other's knees had landed, and inside him was a leaden, despairing blackness. Brown repeated his command, and this time the youngster climbed painfully to his feet, utterly weak and shaky. Gasping, he managed to get out three bitter words: "You—damn—traitor!"

"Aw, hell, you never woulda had a chance anyway!" the other growled, in a coarse attempt at self-justification. "You was game, and I liked that, and I stuck it as long as I seen any hope at all of fighting things through. But when you couldn't get nobody else to sign on, and when Val Meeker started workin' on you in earnest, I seen you was licked. I'm really doin' you a favor, kid, by helping make a short end to your misery!"

Clem demanded heavily, "How much is Val Meeker payin' you to sell me out?"

"Enough! Now—start movin'. Walk ahead of me, and careful!"

There was no alternative. Stumbling and sliding on the loose rock, with his hands shoulder high and no light to aid him, Clem let the traitor herd him down from there, down from the hole-up on the wall of the pocket where mere guns would not have been able to dislodge him. Brown followed without an instant's relaxing of his guard; Clem didn't try to make another break. Presently the ground leveled off beneath his feet and his captor said, "Straight ahead—right out through the entrance."

They walked over uneven ground that tilted upward slightly. Within a few minutes they had cleared the mouth of the pocket and the rolling, night-black range lay empty before them. The wind blew stronger here, unhindered by rocky walls; for a moment the clouds overhead thinned a bit across the face of the moon, so that its radiance shone through in a wide smear and the pattern of scurrying clouds was discernible moving at high speed across the dome of the sky. Then this moment of radiance ended and the dark clamped down more completely than before.

"We'll wait right here," said Brown. "You can lower your hands if you want, but I don't reckon you'll try anything funny."

Clem's arms were beginning to tremble and they ached as he let them drop to his sides. He said nothing; his anger was beyond words. A silence held the pair of them. Through this they presently heard the angry voice of Shorty Jones, in a sputtering torrent of speech. It grew nearer. Shorty was using every resource of a surprisingly complete vocabulary of profanity to tell Chuck Yancey certain details of his low ancestry and his own personal shortcomings; and Yancey's threats had no effect in halting the stream of cussing.

Talley Brown called, "Over this way, Chuck." A moment later the two traitorous Ladder hands had brought their prisoners together, and old Shorty cried, "Then they got you too, Clem? Hod damn the dirty turncoat skunks! I warned you, that first day, you shouldn't of took 'em back—not after they'd once run off with Meeker. But they got me fooled too, I reckon."

"Shut up!" said Chuck Yancey again.

Brown said, "Can you watch both of 'em, Chuck? I'll get the fire going."

They heard him fumble in his pockets; then a sulphur match struck flame, and a moment later the brightness began to strengthen. Turning, Clem saw that a heap of dried brush had been gathered ahead of time, and that Brown had got this to burning.

Wash of flames, dancing in the wind, threw wild shadows as they grew and strengthened. It showed the faces of the four men. Old Shorty was scowling blackly at his betrayers, his upper lip lifted in a snarl of helpless fury. Tally Brown had an unreadable, determined look on his thin features. Clem wondered if he himself looked as sick and lost as he felt. He glanced at Chuck Yancey, saw the broad-faced man look quickly away with a kind of shame.

The bruise on Yancey's jaw showed darkly in the firelight, and Clem suddenly remembered the horse that was supposed to have kicked him. He thought now that he knew how that bruise had actually come about. Chuck Yancey evidently had some small grain of decency in him; it must have taken a little working over with Val Meeker's crushing fists to persuade him to sell out his boss. Yet sell out he had; though now he couldn't look at either Clem or Shorty Jones squarely, in the accusing light of the fire.

And though it went contrary to the grain to beg with these men, Clem had to remember that there was more than himself to think about just then. He said in a tight voice, "Couldn't you leave Shorty out of this? He never hurt you hombres none."

Their faces didn't change. Yancey's scowl only became more set and hard, and Brown growled harshly, "Meeker wants both of you. That was the bargain."

"But for the love of——"

The old man cut him off. "Don't waste your breath on these saddle tramps. Time's up, anyway. Listen!"

Obviously, the lighting of the fire had been a prearranged signal that the treacherous work had been done and the field was open; for now riders were coming in from the darkness. A yell sounded; Talley Brown answered it. After that they swept in at a rush of hoof sound, and quickly the four were surrounded by mounted men on blowing horses. Clem found himself staring straight into the gloating eyes of Val Meeker.

The outlaw's mouth quirked beneath the roached mustache. He piled hard palms on the horn of his saddle and said, "Well, kid? You convinced now I meant what I promised?"

"You couldn't have done it without treachery!" Clem Hardin retorted, anger flaring high in him.

Meeker shrugged. "Oh, I reckon maybe. But this way was the most painless." And then, standing in stirrups, he lifted his head and ran a look about him at the shadowed figures of his men. "All right, you buckos! You know what you got to do! Start moving those cattle into the hills!"

At the command, all but a couple of his riders spurred away toward the hollow and the unprotected stock. Meeker looked back at the four dismounted men.

"Rustle more brush for that fire, Yancey," he ordered briskly. "I got some business to transact with the Hardin kid, and we'll need light." And with the flames leaping higher under the impetus of fresh fuel and driving back the encircling darkness, Val Meeker reached into a pocket of his canvas jacket and brought out a folded paper and shook it open. He stabbed a lean, strong finger at the lines of writing scrawled across the sheet. "You're gonna sign this," he told Clem Hardin flatly.

The boy's blunt jaw clamped hard. He could guess what that paper was. He did not reach to take it; he didn't say a word, but looked squarely into the dark eyes of the other man and waited.

Meeker went on to explain, in a careless tone, "It's a bill of sale for the herd, just so I'll be sure of getting rid of it without any legal trouble. There's a place for the old man to sign as a witness. Put your Xs on there and we'll let you both go—because there won't be anything you can do about it then."

"Damn you!" old Shorty yelped, lifting clenched and trembling fists. "I ain't touchin' my hand to anything that'll help you steal from Ladder iron——"

Val Meeker's answer was simple enough. He merely slipped a foot from stirrup and swung it, hard; the toe of the heavy cowhide boot took Shorty in the face and sent him reeling, to drop on all fours in the dirt. Clem Hardin gave a bellow of rage and, forgetful of everything else, started for the outlaw with the avowed intent of clawing him down from saddle; but Tally Brown's gun, rammed into his ribs, brought him up to a halt, breathing heavily. "If I ever get my hands on you——" he began.

"Don't be a fool!" Meeker snorted. "You punk kid, I beat the tar outta you once and I can do it again as often as you want me to. But if you don't aim to see the old man worked over, you better get to work pronto and start scribbling on this paper. Understand me?"

Clem Hardin understood, and a bleak sense of his own utter helplessness engulfed him. For himself, he could fight them with all the Hardin stubbornness; but it was something else to stand by and watch a loyal old man tortured and beaten, when a couple of words on a piece of paper would spare him.

The resistance went out of him; his shoulders sagged visibly. Across the windy darkness he could hear the cattle in the hollow being pushed to a start from their sheltered grazing ground. Shadows and firelight danced weirdly under the whipping of the chill, wet wind that was heavy with coming rain.

Clem Hardin said, "Give it here!" As he reached his hand to take the paper he felt the first flurry of icy rain-drops, flung with needle sharpness, across his upturned, beaten face.

14

Kate Brophy saw the long-awaited coming of the rain to Kettle Creek country as she was returning from an errand overtown to her tar-paper shack at the edge of Tilden's scattered limits. The cold, needle-sharp sting of it sent her hurrying into the protection of the doorway, and she stood there a moment clutching her cloak nearer about her, listening to rush of wind in the pines behind the building, the drum of the swiftly increasing rain blown against the eaves. Then she pushed open the door and entered.

She heard no sound of breathing, and no instinct spoke to warn her of an alien presence in the narrow room. She closed the door against the gusty outer darkness and felt along the wall to the shelf where she kept a kerosene lamp and matches. Yellow light sprang up, wavered and steadied as she got the wick turned right and set the chimney in place. Then, tossing the blackened twist of matchstick aside, she turned—and saw him.

A gasp broke from Kate. There was something horrible in the stillness of that figure, standing in shadows across the room and regarding her without speech or movement. Cold air poured in through an open window beside him, which must have been his mode of entering the cabin, but the man didn't seem aware of its chill although he was dressed practically in rags. He had no coat; his shirt was torn and filthy, and there was a long rent in one pant leg that caused the garment to flap about him as the streaming wind caught it. He was filthy, emaciated, bearded and the uncertain lamplight showed the dark of clotted blood in his tangled, matted hair.

It was a long, terrible moment before Kate Brophy recognized her husband.

"*Nat!*" She took a step toward him, halted, one hand going up to her throat. "What are you doing here?"

His gaunted features changed shape, twisted into a scowl. "Afraid of your own husband?" he croaked in a voice that didn't sound at all like his own.

"No—no!" she cried hastily. "I was just—startled. They told me you were in the hills, that you were dead——" But she had to force herself to move nearer, because a strange, tangible horror seemed to flow from him, to beat against her. All of a sudden he was grinning, showing all his teeth in a grimace that held no humor; and the yellow lamplight caught a mad glint in his eyes beneath the matted, blood-caked hair plastered against his forehead.

She said faintly: "You're hurt! Sit down and let me get some water heated." But Nat Brophy made no move; stayed the way he was with that awful grin fixed upon her. The lamp flame danced and wavered in the flow of chill night breeze through the window. Kate asked, suddenly remembering, "I thought Luke Sands was with you?"

The grin faded; a frown of puzzlement replaced it. He put up a hand to his head, as though the concentration of thought was physically painful. Then memory darkened his eyes. "Yeah!" he grunted. "Luke Sands—I killed him! He was spyin' on me. I got his gun when his back was turned, and it only took one bullet—— He was against me, like everybody else, like the whole world; everything! Like the trees out there in those damned hills—leaning over me, reaching——" Sweat gleamed on his sunken face as he left off, stood there against the wall panting a little with some nameless emotion.

Kate Brophy, drawing back until the edge of a table stopped her, stared at this man who was her husband and understood. The wound in his head, the privation and horror of wandering about the hills, must have upset in him the shaky balance of unreason; she saw that the crazy, violent streak which she had always feared had now broken all restraints and taken over the battered fortress of Nat Brophy's mind. He was plainly and completely mad——

She wet dry lips with her tongue, fighting panic, wondering what to do with him. "How—how did you find me?" she asked, wanting to keep him talking so she could read the workings of his thoughts. "Who told you where I was?"

"Nobody told me!" he answered triumphantly. "I been following you. I found out for myself where you was hidin'."

"Hiding?" she repeated faintly. "But why should I hide?"

He made a sound that sounded like a laugh but wasn't. "I know! I guess I know what's been goin' on. I been all over this country, watchin' for my chance to kill off the last of them Hardins and finish the whole Satan's brood of 'em. I thought once I *had* killed him, but I guess I missed my shot; because not an hour later I seen the pair of you—you and him—together!"

She couldn't answer him for a moment. He went on, his voice lifting: "I seen him put his hands on you. I seen you touch his face. And I——"

"No! *No!*"

The broken cry ended in a scream, and then Kate Brophy had whirled and was trying to wrench open the door. But her trembling fingers fumbled, trying to raise the latch; and then the man, moving with a quick lunging stride, had reached her. A hand closed upon her arm, jerked her around with ferocious strength. His dirty, bearded face leaned close above her own, the mad eyes glaring at her.

"I seen you standing close to him, your hands on him. I should have killed you right then, both of you. But I wanted it to be one at a time, instead. I wanted to show you I know just what you are and what you been up to behind my back—you cheap——"

Still holding her helpless in that hard, relentless grip, he had reached slowly for the gun tucked into his waist-band—Luke Sands's gun, which had killed Limp Kohler and Luke himself—and he brought it out, his deadly intent showing in his eyes. It dragged desperate words from her, in a rush of frenzy.

"You—you got it wrong, Nat! Honest!" She tried to laugh—a hysterical, babbling sound. "My God, what would I see in a wet-eared kid like Clem Hardin? Why, you must be crazy to. . . ."

It was the wrong word. "I'm *what?* What are you callin' me?" In a frenzy, he began to shake her. He shook her until her bleached hair fell loose about her shoulders. The gun in his hand came up, and she thought he would strike her across the face with its ugly sights.

"Please, Nat!" she moaned hoarsely. *"Please!"*

She had to divert his crazed hatred to another object, and Kate Brophy did it in the only way she knew. "I ain't done anything. Honest! It's that Hardin kid—now that he's boss of Ladder, he thinks he's a man. I didn't know what I was getting into, that day I rode out there. I figured to be nice to him—for your sake, Nat! I asked him if he wouldn't help call the wolves off of you. Instead, he—he said he was gonna see to it you were hanged, because he wanted your homestead and because he wanted—me!

"I didn't know what to do, Nat. I'm scared of him. I

got away the best I could, but I'm scared. I dunno when he might take it into his mind to come after me. He looks like a kid, but he ain't, Nat. He's a devil! You've got to protect me from him!"

It was a fantastic outpouring, but it fed Brophy's natural hatred of Clem Hardin, and Kate saw it take effect. She saw his mad look alter a little; he released her suddenly, and she almost collapsed against the closed door at her back, shaken by violent sobs of relief.

Brophy said, "Where'll I find the skunk? Where'll I notch my sights on him?"

"At Ladder, naturally." She could hardly speak, so choked was she by trembling fright now that the moment of danger was past and the menace shifted, for the moment at least, from herself. A word could undo the structure of lies she had built, turn his ferocious hatred once more full upon her——

His thoughts had headed full-tilt along the new direction she had set for them, however; a sudden consuming impatience seemed to have gripped him. It had him muttering to himself, his dirty fingers squeezing the revolver grips until the knuckles showed white. He took a step toward the door, thrusting Kate out of the way with a sweep of his arm. But then he checked himself and, heeling about, moved instead to the open window. Without another look at her, he bent, shoved a leg across the sill, and quickly slid through.

He was gone then, so abruptly that it began to seem unlikely that he had ever been there—that the terrible, horrifying scene had really taken place. Kate Brophy felt faint all at once, and she groped her way to a chair at the table and dropped into it, hunched there limp from utter exhaustion. The lamp flickered, the rain beat harder against the roof and came with the chill wind through the window. After a moment she heard the quick flurry of a horse's hoofbeats begin and fade out somewhere in the scrub timber behind the shack. . . .

Shorty Jones cried, "Don't do it, kid! Don't sign the thing! Can't you see these snakes don't mean a word they say? Once get your name on that paper and they'll kill us both!"

There was a choking of tears in his voice as he pleaded with the boy. He was down on his hands and knees, where Val Meeker's kick had sent him, and there was a smear of blood on the side of his face that Meeker's heavy boot toe had put there.

"Shut your mouth, damn you!" gritted Talley Brown, and made a threatening gesture with the barrel of his naked gun; but the old cook didn't flinch away from it. His eyes were on his youthful boss, watching fearfully to see what the youngster would do.

Young Clem stood with the bill of sale in his big hands. The paper was already turning damp with the rain that was spearing down steadily now; the brush fire flickered and wavered under its beating, and sparked the individual drops to brightness as Hardin looked through them at Shorty, kneeling by the fire. Numbed as he was to despair, he saw the sense of the old man's warning. He looked around at the outlaws—Brown and Yancey, the two traitors, standing near him, Meeker and the other two sitting horses that were turning restive under the increasing drizzle. One of them was turning up his coat collar, cursing the cold rain.

Looking at Meeker, Clem said heavily, "I reckon he's got it figured out. It don't matter a hell of a lot about me, but it ain't right anything should happen to Shorty Jones. Let me see him walk away from here alive, and I'll sign my name to this. Otherwise, no!"

Val Meeker cut off Shorty's squawk of protest at this

offer. "You ain't makin' no terms here!" he snorted. "I said if you sign, I'd let you both go. You just got to take my word for it."

And the word of Val Meeker was, of course, no assurance at all. Clem stared bleakly at the paper in his hands, the scrawled words running together before his unseeing eyes. Ultimately it made little difference if he signed or not—except that, if he didn't, Meeker would probably lose his temper and start using tough measures of persuasion. Stubbornness would gain him nothing, and might lead to further suffering for old Shorty Jones.

He said dully, "I ain't got a pencil."

"Give him one," Val Meeker ordered shortly.

Chuck Yancey had one. He had to switch his gun to his left hand and dig in his pants pocket with the other, to chase the chewed stub from among the odds and ends stored there. And it was at this moment that the rain suddenly let go with a crash, came barreling down in straight, heavy sheets of water that fell like a battering physical weight.

Involuntary, startled yells broke from the group about the fire. The mounted men found themselves busy suddenly as their horses turned restive and almost got out of hand, feeling the smash of rain. The fire—an impermanent thing of piled brush and juniper sticks—wavered, rallied to the onslaught, and then quite abruptly went out.

Almost without thinking, Clem Hardin grabbed at the slim, desperate chance this offered him. He turned, collided full tilt into the stocky frame of Chuck Yancey. His fists were already swinging; one made contact with solid flesh and bone and the man fell away, and Clem barged on, straight into the curtains of rain that were a faintly luminous silver now in the darkness.

There was no time to think about Shorty Jones, except to hope that the old cook was likewise making use of this moment to escape. Clem couldn't have seen what was happening around him, anyway, in the sudden opaque blackness of the drenching downpour. He heard the shouts, the confusion. A six-gun lanced flame suddenly, its flash and roar drowned by the storm. He plunged ahead, expecting any moment the pound of lead into him. Another gun spoke, twice, but neither bullet came close. Hardin began to feel that he must have thrown his enemies off, that in the mix-up they'd lost his direction and he had a chance to lose them entirely.

And in that instant he floundered into a thick clump of manzanita and stumbled headlong. The spiny branches seemed to cling to him, holding him back as he tried to get his footing and tear free. Then another gunshot smashed above the racket of the storm, aimed apparently at the threshing sound Clem Hardin made in the brush. That bullet did not miss. He felt the solid blow of it somewhere, and the ground came up and struck him.

He was on his side on the wet earth, where the force of the heavy .45 slug had put him. For the moment he felt little pain, only the numbness of shock; but soon enough, he knew, the wound would begin to thaw and the pain would be real enough then—maybe beyond the limits of his endurance. He couldn't tell as to that. He had never been bullet-shot before.

In a daze, these thoughts passed through his mind, and with them the urgent prodding to be up and moving before pain came to render him helpless. If he lay here, his enemies might miss him in the dark and rain, but more likely they would not; and they would be after him, certainly, to try and finish him, if they found that one bullet hadn't done the trick.

With tremendous effort he got his hands under him, palms flat against the hard, wet earth; they seemed like sticks, not a part of his living flesh and without the strength to support him. But he put his weight against them, pushed up, and, getting a boot toe set, lunged staggering up to his feet. His legs were rubbery. He almost stumbled a second time, somehow kept his feet under him, and went slogging forward though his strength was draining rapidly. Consciousness was like a narrowing circle, drawing in closer and closer about him.

The ground seemed to be lifting under him, becoming harder to negotiate. Somewhere ahead, he remembered, on the slope above the pocket where his vigil had been cut short by Talley Brown's betrayal, his saddle gun lay among the rocks and brush. Chances of finding it were negligible, yet it was his one hope of getting his hands on a weapon, and he pinned his waning thoughts on that, even as a hot blur of pain began to force itself upon his attention, growing in intensity and centered somewhere in the region of his shoulder.

Pain swept over him in a blinding tide then; he was struggling through it, trying to keep going, under the obsession of that waiting rifle—— But no, the cold dampness of earth was against his face. He had tripped and fallen without knowing that he fell. Guns were firing somewhere, men shouting, hoofs thudding the earth, and the rain came smashing down in a needling torrent. Clem Hardin made a last futile attempt to force movement into his leaden body. Then everything went away from him in a blanket of foggy nothingness. . . .

Excited voices, and a bobbing light, and hands that pawed at him and tried to turn him over were the next that he knew. He groaned, lifted an arm feebly to ward off the hands. Pain and numbness were in him, and he wanted to be left alone. But they had him on his back, and the light came so close that it put stabs of pain into his squinting eyes. Then somebody cried, "Get that damn lantern out of his face! We can see it's him all right!"

The light retreated to a better distance. And suddenly a new voice joined the others, crying his name over and over. "Clem! Oh, Clem!" Hands that were gentler than the rest touched him—his forehead, his cheek. They tried to lift his head, and then Sally Fox said on a sob, "Oh, God! Look at the blood on him——"

Clem was rousing a little, however; the cold rain against his face helped in this. His fuzzy vision had cleared and he made out the girl on her knees beside him, the legs and lower bodies of the men standing around, and the lantern with streaks of rain spearing across it. Lying motionless like this, the pain was only a dull throbbing, and he tried to tell Sally that. "It don't hurt much," he said. His voice was a sort of mumbling.

Tom Peterson said, "It's his shoulder. Don't look like it's bleeding any more, but it'll have to be taken care of, and there's no way to do that, out here in the rain. He's got to be fetched home, or to the doc—and that real quick."

A considerable amazement in him, Clem twisted his head and focused on the blocky shape of the granger leader. "You, Peterson?" he grunted. "What are you doing here?"

"You can ask Sally about that," said the big man. He sounded disgruntled and embarrassed. "I don't like to be made out a heel, but that's what she done. She got me feeling pretty low about the way us Kettle Creek homesteaders have treated you, Hardin. She come this evening and said she knew you was in trouble with Val Meeker's outfit and that we was a bunch of damn poor neighbors if we'd let you go into it alone. She made things look a mite different to us—shamed us into——"

"Now, don't run yourself down, Tom!" Sally Fox exclaimed, distress in her voice.

"Well, anyway, we got here. Heard some shooting, and when we came riding in they turned their guns on us. It was a pretty bad way to fight—nothin' to shoot at but the flashes. But we busted 'em up and scattered them. And we found Val Meeker dead with a bullet in the neck. You won't need to worry about him any more, kid!"

Leaden disappointment settled in Clem Hardin, tempering the satisfaction of this news. "So when it came to showdown, somebody else had to stomp my snakes!" he muttered. "With me running for my life away through the brush to save my coward hide!" Bitterness twisted its knife in him and he turned his head away, despising himself utterly, wanting to die right there and not face these men who had saved him from the trap made of his own blundering.

But Sally Fox wouldn't listen. "You're gonna make me mad, talking like that! What's cowardly about fighting alone, against men and nature, the way you've done? And don't forget who it was stood up to Meeker, that night at the Green Parrot—you mustn't lose sight of that, Clem! No coward would have done it!"

Somebody muttered, "Speaking of the Green Parrot, we better make a call on Ed Pringle about next—if he ain't already skipped the country before we get to him. Bob Fox done warned him that Kettle Creek wouldn't be needing him and his dive any longer if his pal Val Meeker turned out to be as big a crook as we had him labeled."

"Hardin," said Peterson levelly, "we figure we did ourselves a favor by busting Meeker's gang. And from here on out we want to be friends, if you'll have us. Looks like the drought is broke clean in two, the amount of rain that's coming down right at this minute; but in future we mean to see to it Ladder has access to Kettle Creek. We'll leave gaps in the wire so your cattle can get through to water without endangering our crops.

"Hell, we ain't hogs! But we been so scared of those loud-mouth brothers of yours, and of their tough crew, that we was damned hard to convince you meant to be decent. . . . Will you shake hands, kid?"

The big, strong hand of the Swede thrust at him in the lantern light. Clem looked at it and tried to lift his own arm. He turned white, dropped the arm with a groan. "Sorry!" he gritted. "I——"

Sally cried, "He's too bad hurt to move! Somebody help him onto a horse, will you, please? We've got to get him under a shelter and do something for that hurt shoulder!"

Just then someone came racking up on a blowing bronc. It was Shorty Jones, and he cried sharply, "Who's man enough to come with me and stop the balance of that hellion crew before they get into the foothills with Clem Hardin's cattle? Them that is, get in the saddle—quick!"

"Wait for me, Shorty!" croaked Clem, making a valiant effort to rise. But he sank back, his strength exhausted. The old cook was already gone, pounding away into the rainy darkness. Tom Peterson turned to his followers.

"You heard him! Let's finish this job!" he shouted. "First, though, somebody give me a hand with the kid. You'll have to take care of him, Sally—we still got work ahead of us."

She said quickly, "All I need is to get him on a bronc. I can handle it after that."

"No—no!" Clem's cry of protest was little more than a whimper. A moment later he was being hoisted to his feet, lifted into the saddle of a horse that he knew dimly was his own Ladder-branded sorrel. Somebody threw a slicker across his bent shoulders. A voice said, "Can you clamp your fists around the horn and hang on, kid?"

He wanted to say, "I can ride! Somebody give me a gun and I can at least hold up my end of this fight!" But he couldn't find strength to form the words, and he knew they wouldn't listen to him. Then the men were gone, and there was only the girl, mounted and reining close to his bronc.

"Hang on, Clem! We'll get you there. Everything's going to be all right as soon as you reach the house. We'll take care of you!"

Yes, he thought with the last remnants of conscious, bitter reason, before the jolting of the horse's hoofs sent pain rocking through him. *You'll take care of me! Always, somebody has to. I'll never stand on my own hind legs!*

That hard self-mockery was as far as he got. There was no time then for thinking, or for anything except to hang onto the swaying saddle horn with every remaining ounce of his waning strength.

15

THE STORM seemed to have worn out the worst of its fury. Though the rain continued, in a steady, slogging downpour, it had lessened its force and was no longer coming in heavy, battering sheets to wear down the physical strength of a man in merely holding up his head. This Clement Hardin realized only distantly. He was already as soaked as he well could be, under the cold and clammy slicker. And though the chill touch of the rain helped somewhat to keep consciousness alive in him, the main object of his awareness was the growing pain in his bullet-torn shoulder, and the fatiguing effort of keeping erect between the swells of his saddle.

He had no idea of how long it took to cover the few short miles to Ladder headquarters. He must have lost some of his grip on consciousness in that time, because suddenly he became aware that the slow, hammering rhythm of hoofbeats had halted; that the sorrel was motionless beneath him, and that Sally had dismounted and was pulling at his sleeve, calling to him as she stood close beside his stirrup fender.

"Clem! Listen to me, Clem!" He swung his head with an effort, looked down at her face that was dimly visible through the wet gloom. "We're here. Can you get out of the saddle?"

"Sure," he mumbled gruffly.

But when he tried to lift his right leg free of stirrup, the chore was too much for him and he almost fell bodily to the ground. Sally used both hands to steady him and said hastily, "Let me go in first and get a light made. Then maybe together we can get you inside."

Her footsteps went away from him, slogging across muddy earth and up the soaked planks of the veranda steps. He heard the door open, sticking as it always did in wet weather. Then there was silence but for the steady drip of the rain; and Clem set his mind, as he waited, to gathering his strength against the demand that would be made upon it when Sally returned.

Suddenly another rider was upon him, moving in so unexpectedly that Clem's bronc took fright and shied nervously, almost unseating him. "Kid!" exclaimed a voice tight with fear and excitement. Again a hand was clutching his sleeve; but this time he saw it was Kate Brophy, leaning from her saddle and shaking him as though in a frenzy. "Thank God, kid! I almost missed you. I been waitin' for you to show up, and then in the storm I didn't even see you coming——"

This woman's presence here was a thing holding no meaning. Clem peered through the rain, trying to see her. He stammered, "What—what do you——"

"Brophy's in there, in the house—waiting to kill you. I tell you he's gone crazy, kid—ravin' mad! He's already murdered Luke Sands, up in the hills, and he'd have killed me if I hadn't managed to get rid of him by sendin' him after you instead. I know that was a coward's trick, and I'm sorry—but I at least had nerve enough to follow him and try to warn you."

What she said had only half sunk into his dazed mind, but it filled him with horror. "Wait!" he cried thickly. "You mean——"

"Don't go inside, kid!" she went on wildly. "He's got a gun, don't you understand? Stay out here—gun him down when he shows himself; he ain't nothin' but a mad dog. I don't want to lay eyes on him again—I don't want to see this damned country any longer. I'm heading out of it. Back to Boise, or somewhere. I dunno. You can have that homestead on Kettle Creek, for all I care. I——" She broke off on a long, indrawn breath that was close to a sob of hysteria.

Without another word, she had jerked her horse around and was roweling it insanely, putting it in a mud-spattering gallop along the dark trail to town—a woman who had taken more than she could and had reached her limit in fright and terror. In moments she was gone, out of Clem Hardin's life forever.

But she left behind her a sickening horror that gripped Clem's pain-fevered brain.

Sally! She was in there, alone in that dark house with a madman——

The urgency of need found strength in Clem to get his leg across the saddle, unassisted, but when his boots touched earth he kept going down, flat on his face in the mud. The slicker dropped away, leaving him exposed to the pounding of the rain. The sorrel shifted its hoofs uncertainly, and narrowly avoided stepping on his prone figure with one heavy iron.

But then Clem Hardin had an elbow against the ground and, pushing up, groped with the other hand and hooked the dangling stirrup with it. The sorrel braced itself; the boy put his weight against the stirrup, hauled up to his knees, and from there managed to set one foot into the muddy earth and climb to his feet, using the saddle's horn to steady him. At that instant a choked scream of terror came from the house. A woman's voice. *Sally!*

It could only have been a minute or less since she went into the dark building, to grope through the dark rooms to make a light. It was a matter of seconds longer for Clem Hardin himself to reach the black and gaping doorway. Yet it seemed that time itself dragged at him, held him back. He never knew where he got the strength to carry him the few yards to the veranda steps. He found himself sprawled across them in a stumble, and dragged himself up and went across the rain-whipped boards of the porch on hands and knees, calling Sally's name in a hoarse shout that rasped his throat.

"Clem!" she cried, somewhere in the darkness of the long living room. "There—there's someone in here! He touched my *face!*"

"Get down, Sally!" he shouted at her. "Down on the floor——"

The frightening slap of a gun answered him, the sound room-trapped and punishing to the ears, the flame a quick and lurid stab through the opaque blackness. Brophy had fired at the sound of Clem's voice, and he might have tallied except that Clem was down on his knees and not standing upright. The bullet drilled air above the head of the boy, went out through the open door and was lost. And Clem hurled himself face down across the sill and rolled sideward, driven by an impulse to remove himself as quickly as possible from the spot at which Brophy had aimed.

He came against a leg of the big center table and lay there on his side, trying to suppress the labored sound of his breath and clamp his teeth against the groan of pain that sought to break from him. But with the pressure of the table leg against him, the uncertain darkness had quickly settled itself into the familiar contours of the Ladder living room. Being on his own ground, he knew the shape of the room and the location of every item of furniture as exactly as though he could see them in the dark. Being unarmed, this was the only weapon he had against Nat Brophy's six-gun.

With echoes of that single shot fading, dead silence

came upon the thick darkness, which was broken only by the steady racket of the storm outside. Clem listened for breathing, which might give a clue to the madman's whereabouts, but he couldn't make it out. Suddenly Sally's taut whisper slid out of the shadows, from somewhere in the front corner near the writing desk, or so he judged: "Clem! Are you all right?"

Clem swore silently, but the question didn't bring a shot from the gun. Brophy didn't have it in his crazed mind to try and kill the girl, then—or maybe his supply of bullets was just drawing short and he was hoarding it. Either way, the peril of a hasty shot or a ricochet finding her was sickeningly great. He gritted his teeth, hoping she wouldn't call again. To answer, of course, would be to reveal his position, and that he couldn't do.

But in the meantime he didn't know, either, where Brophy was lurking. Somewhere yonder near the doorway into the hall, he thought from the brief blinding memory of the gun flash. Then, casting about for some way of finding out for sure, he bethought himself of the coat tree that stood near the front entrance—a massive, ugly piece of furniture where shapeless hat and dank, dripping mackinaws and slickers hung and steamed in the heat of the big fireplace during the cold, wet seasons. It was almost in reach of his boot toe as he lay sprawled there upon the floor. Quietly, Clem came up on his elbows and stretched a foot back, groping. He found the base of the rack, reached up a few inches, and hooked his toe around it. With a sudden kick he set it toppling.

The coat tree fell with a crash, its tall shape striking the floor clear out into the center of the room. The gun took the bait; the thunderous roar of it jarred tense nerves and the flash picked out the shapes of the room in a split second of lurid light. Yes, he had placed Brophy correctly—over by the hallway. But the madman, aware that he had revealed himself, was even now ducking back through the doorway; the creak of a floor board, the scrape of clothing against the wall, told of his movement. After all, he didn't know that Clem had no gun.

Clem Hardin knew where there was a gun, however, and he went for it now—hauling himself up against the heavy table and making a staggering lunge toward the fireplace, where his groping hands felt for and located the cold round barrel of the rifle that always hung there. He took it down; it felt tremendously weighty, but he braced it against his hip and then had to lean against the rough stones of the fireplace for a moment, summoning his strength. He said a small prayer: *God, you got to let me keep goin'—Sally's in danger, with that nut loose in here!* After that he lurched forward, reached the wall, got a shoulder against it, and slid his weight along that way until he was looking into the long hallway that split the back of the house, from living room to kitchen.

It seemed darker yet in there, if that was possible. The air was stale, trapped by the close walls and tanged with the stink of those two revolver shots. Doors opened off it —to closets, to storerooms, to the tiny office, and to the narrow stairway leading to bedrooms on the second floor. Clem Hardin, of course, knew every inch of it, but there was something rather horrible in the thought of venturing into that narrow gut of blackness, in stalking a crazed Nat Brophy through the dark labyrinth of the rambling Ladder ranch house.

He had one shell in his rifle. If that was Luke Sands's gun Brophy had, then it, too, must be nearly empty by now. Sands had killed Limp Kohler with it, and then— according to what Kate had told him—Brophy had used it to kill Sands. He had already fired it twice in the last five minutes. That left two bullets, unless Brophy might have used them to bring down game while he was wandering the hills. In fact, the gun might even now be empty.

But he mustn't count on that. He had to figure at least two shells left to Brophy. And, facing those two bullets against his one, he stepped through the doorway and into the stale warmth of the hall.

A board creaked toward the rear of the corridor and nervous reflex almost cramped his finger on the trigger; but he held the motion, frozen in position, listening for other sounds. None came. He could imagine the crazy man waiting back there for him to betray himself with a shot. Under the soaked and clammy clothing, sweat was working down his ribs. His right hand, at the trigger guard, was slick with sweat and beginning to tremble badly. His legs were turning rubbery again, from weakness.

He tried another step. As he set boot to floor the big, blunt-roweled spur clinked with a sound as sharp and violent as a chime. And at once Nat Brophy worked his six-gun, triggering point-blank down the throat of the hall.

But Clem was pulled over close to the corridor wall, and the bullet only grazed him, to bury itself in the plaster somewhere behind him. And on the tail of the deafening shot he threw off his only shell, a snap shot with the rifle against his thigh and his target the faintly limned shape of Brophy—wild-eyed, bloody, disheveled—that the brief flash of that other gun's muzzle flare had shown him.

The two shots mingled in the dark slot of the hallway. Clem Hardin heard a dreadful sound from the recovered darkness ahead of him—something between a groan and a cough. He heard Sally's sharp scream, out in the living room. Then the recoil of the rifle had thrown him hard against the wall at his back, against his hurt shoulder. The rifle fell from nerveless fingers, and he knew he was falling, sliding down the wall to slump half-conscious at the foot of the baseboard.

There was a strange kind of peace in lying like that, his body numbed beyond pain and the dim realization in him of a terrific pressure removed. From the sounds that Nat Brophy made as the bullet struck—and the utter silence that lay now upon the far end of the hall—he judged that Brophy must be dead. Brophy, the killer of his brothers Japheth and Noah. . . . That was justice, he supposed—a sort of primitive correctness, the blood debt being exacted by the lone surviving member of the Hardin line. But in the awful moment itself, he hadn't thought about that at all.

Even now it didn't seem to matter much. To him, Brophy had been some horrible kind of mad and dangerous animal that must be destroyed before he could bite someone else and infect them, too, with death . . . before he could do harm to Sally. That was all Clement Hardin had cared about, and now he was ready to rest, not concerned that he lay in a bloody heap on the hard boards of the hallway, with powder stench in his nostrils and a dead man sprawled in the dark not a dozen feet away.

But now there was a light, and Sally Fox came with the lamp she had found and managed to set burning. With a sob of horror she dropped to her knees beside Clem, and set the flickering lamp on the floor and took the boy's head into her arms, against her round young breast, and began hugging him and covering his face with scared and frantic kisses. "Oh, Clem!" she cried, like a hurt child, over and over. "Don't die! You ain't gonna die!"

Half smothered under the sudden avalanche of affection, Clem Hardin lifted a hand in feeble protest. "Your hair," he grunted. "It tickles——"

Gone quickly red, she drew back and tossed her brown curls back across her shoulders. But it was mostly a great relief that the lamplight showed in her pretty face. "He didn't hit you? Oh, thank God, Clem!" Immediately efficient, she leaned and slipped his arm around her shoulders, unmindful of the blood that came from his wet clothing and smeared her hands and the slicker she wore. "I'll help you up, Clem. Just one more effort—we'll get you into the other room and onto the sofa, and then you can rest while I get some hot water and see what I can do about your shoulder. Now, come on, darling—please!"

He put his best effort into doing everything she wanted of him, docilely. Leaning heavily on her, he got to his feet somehow, and they went swaying and staggering out of the hallway and into the living room again, and there Sally guided Clem to the old horsehair sofa, which sagged with broken springs, and got him upon it. As he lay there gasping a little, she went back for the lamp and set it on the table, and then she was beside him again, her strong hands smoothing his hair and stroking his cheek as though she couldn't have enough of the wonder of touching him and finding him still warm with life. He heard her voice, felt the breath of her words soft against his ear as she leaned above him.

"I guess you see now who was right! My pop and me, we knew all along you hadn't no business talking about yourself the way you always do. You think you're a coward, that you can't stand up and fight a man's fight? But look at what you just did—and you did it for me! That's what I'll remember, Clem!" Her lips trembled; he could feel them, brushing his cheek. "Even if you don't seem to know I'm alive, I'll always be able to look back and know that there was one time when I was in trouble and you cared enough to—to——"

The words broke off, and suddenly Sally was on her feet and hurrying away. Clem tried to raise himself, to call after her; but then he fell back again to the sofa, weak and limp. He was smiling a little.

She wasn't running away from him. She would be back, with clean cloths and water and whatever she could find, to work on his hurt shoulder. He would tell her, then, all that was in his full and bursting heart. He lay there, forming the words, and listened to the rain that walked across the dark world outside the house.

He was Clement Hardin, owner of the Ladder iron. He had gone through the storm and earned a deep and certain confidence in himself. He wouldn't be losing it again.

D(wight) B(ennett) Newton is the author of a number of notable Western novels. Born in Kansas City, Missouri, Newton went on to complete work for a Master's degree in history at the University of Missouri. From the time he first discovered Max Brand in Street and Smith's *Western Story Magazine*, he knew he wanted to be an author of Western fiction. He began contributing Western stories and novelettes to the Red Circle group of Western pulp magazines published by Newsstand in the late 1930s. During the Second World War, Newton served in the U.S. Army Engineers and fell in love with the central Oregon region when stationed there. He would later become a permanent resident of that state and Oregon frequently serves as the locale for many of his finest novels. As a client of the August Lenniger Literary Agency, Newton found that every time he switched publishers he was given a different byline by his agent. This complicated his visibility. Yet in notable novels from *Range Boss* (1949), the first original novel ever published in a modern paperback edition, through his impressive list of titles for the Double D series from Doubleday, *The Oregon Rifles, Crooked River Canyon*, and *Disaster Creek* among them, he produced a very special kind of Western story. What makes it so special is the combination of characters who seem real and about whom a reader comes to care a great deal and Newton's fundamental humanity, his realization early on (perhaps because of his study of history) that little that happened in the West was ever simple but rather made desperately complicated through the conjunction of numerous opposed forces working at cross purposes. Yet, through all of the turmoil on the frontier, a basic human decency did emerge. It was this which made the American frontier experience so profoundly unique and which produced many of the remarkable human beings to be found in the world of Newton's Western fiction.